W9-DGO-253

# Contents

# MEGA SCARY STORIES
## FOR SLEEP-OVERS

**By Don Wulffson**
**Illustrated by Dwight Been**

Lowell House
Juvenile
Los Angeles

CONTEMPORARY BOOKS
Chicago

*For Barbara Schoichet—a gifted editor who works "monsterously" hard.*
*—D.W.*

*To all my friends who consented to pose as my monsters.*
*—D.B.*

Copyright © 1996 by RGA Publishing Group, Inc.
Published by Price Stern Sloan, Inc.,
A member of The Putnam & Grosset Group, New York, New York.

Printed in the United States of America. Published simultaneously in Canada. All rights reserved. No part of this publication may be reproduced, stored in a retrieval system or transmitted, in any form or by any means, electronic, mechanical, photocopying, recording, or otherwise, without the prior written permission of the publisher.

ISBN 0-8431-8219-9
First Edition
3 5 7 9 10 8 6 4

**Library of Congress Cataloging-in-Publication Data**

Wulffson, Don
    Mega scary stories for sleep-overs / by Don Wulffson:
illustrated by Dwight Been.
        p. cm.
    "An RGA book."
    Summary: A collection of scary short stories, including "Death Sight," "Fountain of Horror," and "Brain Pictures."
    ISBN 0-8431-8219-9
    1. Horror tales, American. [1. Children's stories, American.
2. Horror stories. 3. Short stories.] I. Been, Dwight, ill.
II. Title
PZ7.W96373Me 1996
[Fic]–dc20                                          95–51074
                                                         CIP
                                                         AC

Based on a design by Michele Lanci-Altomare

# The Corpse of Mr. Porter

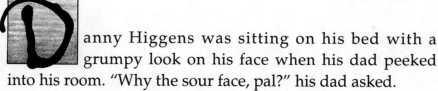anny Higgens was sitting on his bed with a grumpy look on his face when his dad peeked into his room. "Why the sour face, pal?" his dad asked.

"Just bored," Danny replied. "Tonight's Halloween, and I can't think of anything fun to do. I mean, I'm thirteen. I'm getting tired of the old trick-or-treating bit."

His dad looked thoughtful. "Well, when I was a kid we used to pull pranks."

"*You*—Roansboro's very own deputy sheriff?" Danny raised an eyebrow in disbelief. "Like, what kind of stuff did you do?"

"Oh, like hiding in the bushes, then jumping out at trick-or-treaters when they came by."

"Dad, that is *sooooo* lame!" Danny said with a laugh.

"But we also did some good stuff. Like one time a couple of my buddies and I—" He chuckled. "Well, never mind. I shouldn't be telling you these things. It really doesn't set a good example."

"Doesn't matter, anyway," Danny said with a smile. "I mean, I'm sure back in the old days they seemed fun, but they're probably lame."

"Could be," his father said, looking a little hurt.

"Still, you *are* cool to admit that you were once a kid too, and liked to mess around once in a while," Danny admitted. "But that still doesn't solve my problem. You and Mom are going to a party. Sheryl is having a sleep-over. And me, I've still got nothing to do."

"Hey, Dad!" Danny's older sister Sheryl hollered from downstairs. "Where's my sleeping bag? I can't find it!"

"Be right down, honey!" he called back, heading out of Danny's room. "Don't worry, guy," he said over his shoulder. "You'll figure out something to do."

As his dad tromped downstairs to help Sheryl, Danny wandered out of his room and looked over the railing. His sister was lugging things into the den where her sleep-over was going to be. "Well, one thing I know I'm going to do is get out of the house," Danny muttered. "Imagine, a den full of goofy girls!"

And then it suddenly hit him—the Halloween prank of the century!

He raced to the phone to call his best friend, Steve Riley. "Come over to my house as soon as you can," he said excitedly, the second Steve picked up the phone. "I've got the coolest idea for something to do for Halloween."

"What? Ring people's doorbells and ask for candy?" Steve asked sarcastically.

"Just come on over," Danny said, ignoring him. "And bring that mask you have that looks like a corpse's face. We're gonna scare some girls to *death* tonight!"

............

"So, what's the plan?" Steve asked, tossing a rubber fright mask to Danny, who was sitting on the front porch waiting for him.

"It's going to be the coolest!" Danny exclaimed. "Tonight Sheryl is having a sleep-over with a bunch of geeky girls. They're going to watch horror flicks and tell scary stories."

"How wimpy," Steve said, rolling his eyes. "So where do we come in?"

Danny took a deep breath. "Remember when old Mr. Porter died of a heart attack last week?"

"Yeah, they buried him yesterday," Steve said.

"Well, who do I look like?" Danny asked, holding the rubber mask to his face, covering his mischievous grin.

Steve squinted as he stared, then burst out laughing. "That mask *does* look like Mr. Porter! I can't believe I never noticed it before. And with a few little changes, we could—"

"You got it!" Danny snickered. Then he quickly quieted down and looked around. Inside the house he could hear his mom and sister yakking away about the sleep-over. His dad was washing the car in the driveway, but was still within earshot. "We wait until my sister and her friends are telling their stupid horror stories, and when they're already a little creeped out . . . *Mr. Porter* will crash their party!"

Steve rubbed his chin in thought. "You know, since they buried him last week, it just might work." Then his brow furrowed. "But there's two of us. Which one of us is going to be Mr. Porter? I mean, you can if you want. But what am I supposed to do?"

"I don't know," Danny admitted. "Maybe you can be in charge of sound effects. You know, make weird noises or something." He shrugged and got up from the porch. "Let's go get the costume ready. We'll figure out the details as we go along."

. . . . . . . . . . .

Steve and Danny found most of what they needed in the attic, including some dusty old clothes, a moth-eaten wig, and even a pair of old-fashioned spectacles just like the kind Mr. Porter had worn. Next, while Danny modeled the mask, Steve applied some of the makeup Danny had "borrowed" from his mother. He used bluish green eye shadow to give the mask just the right decomposed look, and with brown eyeliner he created a bunch of moles on the cheeks, just like the real ones Mr. Porter had had.

"Wow, you really look like a dead guy, Danny!" Steve exclaimed, examining his work. "Look at yourself," he added, with an evil chuckle as he held up a dirty, cracked mirror in front of Danny. "You look like a regular zombie!"

Danny snickered as he looked at himself. Then he put on the old clothes they'd selected—a dark suit full of moth holes, a long-sleeved shirt that had once been white but was now pale yellow with age, and a tie that looked at least a hundred years old. When he added the dusty wig Danny whooped with delight, and the two boys proclaimed their work a success.

"Wow," Danny exclaimed. "I almost feel dead in this getup!" And then he suddenly broke into a fit of sneezing and coughing. "Boy, this stuff sure is musty."

"Well, even though you get to have most of the fun," Steve replied, "I'm glad it's you wearing all those stinky, dusty clothes and not me."

Danny started to make a comment but could only reply with a huge sneeze, followed by a fit of coughing. Quickly he took off the mask, wig, and clothes, setting them in a pile, ready for that night. "Let's get out of here," he said, clambering over piles of old junk toward the attic door. "I'm starting to feel all itchy." He gave the door a pull. "Oh, great," he muttered. "Hey, Steve, give me a hand. The door's jammed."

Together the boys gave the old door a hard yank, then another. Finally, on the third try it rattled open, and the two made their way down from the attic and into the hallway.

"What's going on?" Danny's mom asked. She was just coming up the stairs from the living room and had stopped, looking at the two boys suspiciously. "What are you guys up to?"

"Oh, nothing, Mom," Danny said, quickly putting on his most innocent-looking face.

"We were just getting ready for trick-or-treating, Mrs. Higgens," Steve added, also wearing the face of an angel. "There's some pretty funky stuff in your attic."

"Yeah, but we didn't find anything, though," Danny lied. "Guess we'll just have to paint our faces like we did last year, right Steve?"

Steve nodded. "Looks like you're right, Danny," he said, trying not to smile. "It's just going to be another boring old Halloween."

...........

That night, as soon as it started turning dark, the doorbell rang non-stop and gangs of trick-or-treaters paraded to the Higgens' front door. For the first hour, in between getting ready for their party, Danny's mom and dad dropped handfuls of candy into the goodie bags of every goblin, ghost, and witch that dropped by.

Danny left for Steve's at 6:30 P.M. He told his parents they planned to check out a dance at the school, but instead they sat in Steve's bedroom fine-tuning their plans.

Sheryl's friends began arriving for the sleep-over at 7:00, and when her parents left for their party at 8:00, the girls took over handing out candy to the last few trick-or-treaters. Then, making a huge batch of popcorn, they retreated to the den with sodas and leftover candy to watch a horror movie. After screaming until they were hoarse, the girls turned off the movie and the lights, then snuggled into their sleeping bags and began telling spooky stories.

Sheryl's story was pretty good, and so was Linda Hazama's and Chondra Johnson's. But Maggy Olivares told the scariest and weirdest story of all. She was in the middle of one about people who had tiny spiders growing out of their skin when Sheryl interrupted her.

"Shush, everyone," Sheryl whispered. "I thought I just heard something in the house." She got up and peeked out the door of the den. "Nobody there," she announced over her shoulder, "but I could've sworn I heard someone come in the back door."

"We'd better go check it out," Maggy suggested.

Traveling in a huddle, the girls checked all the doors and were relieved to find each one securely locked. Then they went from room to room, finding no sign of anyone.

"Guess it was just my imagination," Sheryl said as they returned to the den.

"Well, I hope so!" Jessica Warner exclaimed. She was the youngest of the group, and her quavering voice let everyone know she was still a little shaken.

"My story was probably just freaking you out," Maggy assured Sheryl. Then she looked at everyone else. "Now, can I finish my story, or is everyone too scared?"

"Sure, finish it," Linda said, trying to sound brave. "Halloween's about getting scared, isn't it?"

Nervously the girls sat down on their sleeping bags, and Maggy went on with her story. She was just at the creepiest part—about a gadzillion tiny spiders crawling out of someone's ear—when she suddenly stopped herself. "Now *I'm* hearing something!" she exclaimed.

All the girls' eyes had gone wide with fear, for they, too, had heard a weird thumping noise coming from somewhere in the house.

For a moment, all was silent. Then came the thumping again, this time accompanied by a hollow banging noise. Somewhere overhead came the sound of heavy footsteps.

"Somebody *is* in the house!" Chondra cried.

"Let's get out of here!" Linda wailed.

"Calm down," Sheryl said firmly. "I'll call my folks." Her hands trembling, she dialed the number her parents had given her before they left. After the first ring a woman came on the line, and Sheryl quickly babbled her story into the phone. Every eye was on her as she slowly hung up.

"My parents already left the party," Sheryl told the frightened girls looking at her. "They left before I even called. I mean, it's not even ten o'clock. Why would they leave so early? It doesn't make—"

Suddenly Jessica's bloodcurdling shrieks filled the room, and Linda, standing next to her, nearly fell over Maggy and Chondra as they clutched each other in horror. Sheryl's mouth was wide open mid-scream, and she was backing away, pointing.

There, in the window, was the rotted face of a corpse pressed up against the glass. Its mouth was moving, exposing blackened, decayed teeth, and Sheryl could hear muffled cries tearing from its throat.

"It's . . . it's Mr. Porter!" Chondra cried, as a withered hand with long, twisted fingernails clawed at the glass.

"But he's dead!" Jessica shrieked.

"Not anymore," Linda said, her eyes bulging. "He—"

Sheryl doubled over laughing. "It's not old man Porter!" she exclaimed. "It's just my stupid brother!"

Suddenly the face vanished.

"Your brother?" Chondra gasped.

"Yeah," Sheryl replied. "It's got to be him. Mom overheard him and his friend Steve trying to figure out what to do tonight. I guess the jerks decided to scare us."

Upstairs the pounding began again, and suddenly there were yells and cries followed by the sound of shattering wood. The girls huddled together and screamed, and then came a weak knocking on the front door.

"Don't open it!" Jessica cried.

"It's just my dumb brother," Sheryl insisted. Trying to collect herself, she took a deep breath, opened the front door . . . and all the girls screamed at once.

Standing there was the corpse of Mr. Porter. His skin was a greenish color, and he was wearing a dark suit.

"I'm so cold," the corpse hissed. "Help me."

"Get out of here, Danny!" Sheryl scoffed.

"Please help me," the corpse begged.

"Get lost!" Sheryl yelled. Then she slammed the door and turned to face her still-terrified friends. "I'm telling you it was Danny," she said. "It had to have been. His friend Steve is probably out there too. He probably—"

But Sheryl's mouth dropped open before she could finish, and all she could do was stare in shock and disbelief. Coming down the stairs were . . . Danny and Steve!

"Why wouldn't you let us out?" Danny asked. "Didn't you hear us banging and yelling to you?"

Sheryl looked back and forth from the front door to the boys. "Wh-what are you talking about?" she stammered.

"We were going to scare you," said Danny, holding up the rubber mask in his hand. "We sneaked into the house while you and your friends were watching that scary movie, and we went up into the attic to get the old clothes I was going to wear. Steve was going to make creepy noises upstairs, and I was going to crash your little party dressed up like the corpse of Mr. Porter."

"But the attic door jammed," Steve explained. "We couldn't get out, and finally we had to break it down."

"B-but, then who—or what—was just outside?" gasped several of the girls at once.

"What are you talking about?" Danny asked.

In bits and pieces, the girls all told different parts of what had happened. When they were through, Danny and Steve were both laughing.

"Well," Danny said, "sounds to me like somebody else had the same idea we did."

"But they beat us to it," Steve complained. "How crummy. We end up locked in the stupid attic while somebody else has all the fun!"

Just then lights flashed across the windows as a car pulled into the driveway. A moment later Mrs. Higgens hurried through the door, forgetting to close it in her rush.

"How come you're home so early?" Sheryl asked, still a little shaky.

"We got worried," her mother said. "Didn't you hear?"

"What?" Danny and Sheryl asked, almost in unison, as the other kids gathered around.

"All the sheriff's deputies—your dad included—were called to the station to go out on patrol. And just about everybody else at the party left when we heard the news."

"What news?" Sheryl asked, a chill creeping up her spine.

"I don't want to frighten any of you kids, but over at the cemetery one of the graves was opened. It was Mr. Porter's grave, and his body is missing. Either somebody dug up his corpse or—"

"Or what?" all the kids pleaded at once.

Mrs. Higgens suddenly looked very uncomfortable. "Well," she began, "some people think maybe he was buried alive—by accident, of course—and that he, well, that he . . . "

"Mom!" Danny screeched as the whole house erupted in screams of abject horror. "Behind you!"

Coming through the still-ajar door was the dirt-covered, moldering corpse of Mr. Porter. "Why . . . wouldn't . . . you . . . let . . . me . . . in?" it asked. "I'm . . . soooooo . . . cold!"

"Oh, I'm sorry. Come here and let me warm you up," Mrs. Higgens said matter-of-factly as she wrapped her arms around Mr. Porter's corpse and gave it an affectionate hug. Then she smiled and looked at the hideous face. "Hi, honey," she said, kissing one of the ghastly looking cheeks.

"Huh?" Danny and Sheryl gasped, gagging with disgust . . . as their dad pulled off a very realistic mask.

"It was your parents all along!" Chondra exclaimed.

"Totally cool!" Maggy cried, with a nervous laugh. "Your parents pulled off the ultimate Halloween prank!"

"I've never been so freaked!" Steve said, struggling to get his breath. He turned to Danny. "They must've heard us when we were making our plans."

"Yeah," Danny said, his face still white as a sheet.

"Pretty good for a couple of old fogies, huh?" his mom said with a mischievous grin.

"Hope I didn't scare you too much, pal," his dad added, giving Danny a wink. "I just didn't want you to think your father was—what was the word you used?"

" 'Lame,' " Danny murmured, his face reddening as he looked around at everybody. "But who's the real lamebrain now?" he joked, mocking himself. Then slowly an impish look came over him. "But I've got a whole year to figure out how I'm going to get even!" And along with all the others, he burst out laughing.

# Death Sight

hey made fun of Molly Lund. It wasn't just that she was very tall for her thirteen years, or that she was stoop-shouldered, or even that she didn't wear very stylish clothes. No, it was her eyes. That's what freaked out her classmates and made just about everyone who met her uncomfortable. Yes, it was Molly Lund's eyes—one blue and one brown—that disturbed people the most. That and the fact that she had trouble smiling. It was hard to smile when you knew the things that Molly knew, saw the things that Molly saw.

Things had been bad in grade school in New Jersey. But they were even worse at Tecumseh Middle School in Gilson Falls, Idaho, where Molly and her parents had moved to last year. The kids in Gilson Falls acted like monsters toward Molly. She tried to make friends, to be nice to everyone and fit in. That's all she wanted. But the kids still treated her like an outcast, a freak. They made fun of her, tormented her, and worst of all, they used her.

"Oh, Mollll—eeee," Courtney Harris called out as Molly arrived at school early one morning.

"Hey, eggbrain, get over here!" Rita Strimpus ordered. "You can't hide from us!"

Hugging her books to her chest, Molly looked over to where Courtney and Rita were hanging out with their usual low-life crowd. Jason Parks, Nan Banks, Hank Jones, Dave Carlton, and Lydia North—the whole rotten bunch of them were lounging around by the gym. Their only goals in life seemed to be picking on kids and making life miserable for every teacher who had the misfortune of having them in one of their classes.

"What are you waiting for?" Hank demanded. "Didn't you hear what Rita told you?"

Molly knew it was useless to ignore them. She knew exactly what they wanted, and she knew she would have to give it to them. Her head hanging, Molly slowly made her way over to the tough-looking group.

"Hi," she said shyly. "What do you want?"

"You know what we want," Nan said with a sneer. "The answers to the history test we're having today. We know you know what they are, so tell us."

"And don't bother giving us the questions," Courtney added. "It's multiple choice, so just tell us the answers." She batted her overly made-up eyes. "You know, A, B, C, D—but no F's. We can get F's on our own!

18

Everyone burst out laughing. Everyone but Molly, that is. She was busy contemplating whether or not she should make a run for the classroom. But she knew that one way or another, she'd still have to deal with them later. So she might as well get it over with.

"We're waiting . . ." Rita said, clicking her ballpoint pen and opening the palm of her hand, ready to write down all the answers.

With a sigh, Molly took out a spiral binder, and read the correct answers to the thirty multiple-choice questions that would be on the test. Courtney, Rita, and the others busily made out their various crib sheets. Not one of them noticed that the page Molly had randomly turned to in her notebook was completely blank.

...........

When Molly and her folks had first moved to Gilson Falls, the other kids had thought she was the class brain. She always got A's, always aced every test. It was Courtney who had first realized that Molly wasn't just smart, but that she had some special knack for getting the answers. And it was Courtney who decided that the strange, dark-haired girl with the mismatched eyes should use her special abilities to help Courtney and her friends—or else.

Back in New Jersey not so many of her classmates had figured out about Molly's "seeing powers." Maybe they were too young, or maybe it was because the grade school she'd attended had been a lot larger than Tecumseh Middle School, and she hadn't stood out as much. At any rate, the kids just didn't seem quite so mean back in grade school, and the few kids who had used her at least pretended to be her friend to get what they wanted.

But not in Gilson Falls. Bullying was how Courtney and her bunch got what they wanted, and when Molly had tried to hold out on them, the consequences had been painful and sometimes terrifying. Oh, there had been the usual nastiness of kids tripping her in the hall or filling her locker with garbage. But when a rock had crashed through her bedroom window one night with a note attached that threatened not only her but her parents, Molly had to give in.

Not telling her parents about what was going on, and claiming she had no idea who'd thrown a rock through the window, Molly decided that from then on she would do whatever Courtney and her gang wanted. It did stop the attacks, but unfortunately it didn't stop the torment.

"Hey, guys, look who's here," a familiar voice exclaimed loudly the following day, just outside the cafeteria.

Molly was sitting on a bench by herself, eating from her sack lunch. The screechy voice coming from behind her was Courtney's. Molly also heard three people giggling, and without having to turn around, she knew that the goons with Courtney were Rita, Lydia, and Jason.

"Great," she muttered to herself. "Not again!"

"Good golly, if it isn't Miss Molly!" Rita exclaimed with a nasty chuckle.

"Hiya, Molly, ol' pal," Lydia said, plunking down on the bench and waving a paper in front of Molly's face. "Look, egghead, it's my history test. Guess what grade I got!"

"You got an A," Molly said softly. "You *all* got A's."

"Know what?" Lydia turned to her friends with a smirk. "I think I'll throw a party this weekend to celebrate our

20

good grades. And I think I'll invite everyone . . . except one person. Guess who that is, Molly," she said, making a sad clown face and fixing her gaze on the poor tortured girl.

"Why are you so cruel?" Molly asked, her one blue eye and one brown eye blinking back tears.

"Us, cruel?" Rita asked. With the expression of an angel on her face, she looked around at her friends. "Do you think we're cruel, guys?"

"No," Jason replied, "but I *do* think it was really mean of Molly to say such a thing." He shrugged and gave Molly a crooked grin. "But I'll forgive you, brainiac. After all, you did help us out on our tests, so I guess you can't be *all* bad."

Molly just looked at him.

"By the way, Mol," Jason went on. "Tell me, what's your secret? How *do* you get the test answers ahead of time?"

"You wouldn't understand," Molly replied. "Even I don't really under—"

"I wouldn't understand, huh?" Jason snarled. "You sayin' I'm stupid or something?"

"No," Molly said uncomfortably.

"Then tell us how you get the answers," Lydia demanded. "Tell us *now!*"

"It—it's better that I don't," Molly stammered.

"Well, I happen to disagree," Courtney said, her eyes narrowing. "In fact, I think it's better that you *do*. And if you don't, then some pretty rotten things might just start to happen to you."

The whole group closed in on Molly, as if emphasizing Courtney's threats.

"Believe me, you really don't want me to tell you," Molly warned. "Especially not right now."

"And why's that?" Rita scoffed.

"Because if I did, Ms. Pelson and Mr. Jones, the new vice-principal, would overhear," Molly said simply.

All the kids looked around. There were a few kids eating their lunches outside the cafeteria, but most were inside, and there wasn't a grown-up in sight.

"Are you nuts?" Lydia asked. "How're they supposed to hear us when they're not even—"

She stopped what she was saying as Rita suddenly tapped her on the arm and pointed over her shoulder. Just at that moment, from around the corner of the cafeteria, Ms. Pelson and Mr. Jones appeared. They were walking slowly, very slowly, and paying keen attention to Molly and the group around her. For a moment they stopped, glanced suspiciously at Courtney and her gang, then continued on their way.

"How did you know they were coming?" Courtney demanded, once the two adults were out of earshot. "And how did you know they were spying on us?"

Molly didn't reply.

"She must've *seen* them coming," Jason insisted, not sounding very certain. "I mean, how else could she have possibly known?"

...........

Later that day, Molly slid into her seat in her science class, her last class of the day. Jason, Lydia, and Courtney were also in the class, and the three of them straggled in, late as usual, plunking down at their desks behind Molly.

After scolding the three for coming in tardy, Mr.

Angellini grinned at the class. "OK, everybody, I've got a surprise for you. Put your books under your desks, take out a pen, and get ready for a . . . pop quiz!"

"How come you didn't tell us there'd be a pop quiz?" Courtney hissed at Molly.

"Yeah, egghead held out on us!" Jason whispered angrily to Lydia.

"There was no need to tell you anything," Molly replied quietly, looking back at the three snarling kids over her shoulder. "Just wait and see."

"Today's pop quiz will be on all of the material we discussed yesterday," Mr. Angellini announced to the class as he clicked open his briefcase. "It'll be on crustaceans and other forms of—"

"What's that?" Courtney demanded, leaning forward as close as she could to Molly.

"You don't need to know," Molly whispered.

"Huh?" Courtney grunted.

"There won't be a quiz," Molly replied.

Sure enough, just then Mr. Angellini's face turned red as he was rummaging through his briefcase. "Darn," he grumbled. "I can't seem to find the questions for your quiz." He looked at the class and forced a smile. "I know you'll all be disappointed, but it looks like there won't be a test today after all."

Instantly sighs of relief and whoops of joy erupted in the classroom.

"How'd you know?" Courtney whispered to Molly, a bewildered look on her face.

"You mean about his car?" Molly replied evenly.

"What's it got to do with his—" Courtney began.

23

"I must have left the quiz sheets in my car," Mr. Angellini said with a shrug. "Oh well, this will give you time to study tonight."

...........

After class, Courtney, Jason, and Lydia cornered Molly in front of school as she was leaving to walk home.

"What gives with you?" Jason demanded, his voice a bit unsteady. "You're some kind of freak, aren't you?"

"Yeah, you know everything that's about to happen," Lydia said, as if making an accusation. "I mean, it's like you can see the future or something."

"You *do* see the future, don't you?" Courtney asked.

Molly nodded shyly.

"How?" Courtney demanded. "How do you know what's coming?"

Molly shrugged. "I don't know," was all she said.

The three bullies stared at her. Then a wicked smile came across Courtney's face. "If you know the future, can you change it?" she asked.

It was at that very moment that Molly suddenly heard the squeal of metal on metal. Then she *saw* and heard the shattering of wood. The sounds and sights were all in her head, and soon she saw faces filled with terror. There was a lot of red everywhere, too. Shuddering, Molly realized it was blood. She blinked several times, trying to bring herself back to the moment. That's when she heard Courtney practically screaming at her.

"Well, *can* you?" Courtney was demanding. "Can you change the future?"

Molly didn't answer. She turned and walked away, leaving the threesome gawking at her back.

"Where do you think you're going, freak?" Courtney shouted after her.

But Molly just kept walking. Courtney, as Molly knew she would, stood glowering in anger and confusion, but she didn't make an attempt to follow. For Molly knew something else too—Courtney was scared.

···········

As always, Courtney and her group went to their favorite hangout after school, an abandoned old shack down by the railroad tracks. Long ago it had been the railroad's signal station. Now, however, the place was nothing more than a moldering, dilapidated hovel, its clapboard walls warped and twisted by age and weather.

"I don't buy any of this ESP junk," Nan said as she took a long swig from a can of soda.

"Then how does she do it?" Jason wanted to know. "I mean, it's like she sees *everything* in advance."

"Gotta be some kind of trick," Nan replied as Hank nodded in agreement.

"Then how'd she know about Mr. Angellini leaving the copies of the quiz in his car?" Jason asked.

"She probably just heard him talking before class," Dave suggested.

"Nah, you weren't there," Courtney said. "Mr. Angellini *himself* didn't know he'd left the quiz sheets in his car until he was in the classroom and had already announced the quiz! I mean, he was totally surprised and embarrassed."

"It's absolutely got to be the seeing into the future thing," Lydia decided.

"I think it's got something to do with those weird eyes of hers," Jason said. "You know how they're two different colors—maybe that's what gives her the power."

"All I know is she gives me the creeps," Rita said with a shudder. "I think—" Suddenly Lydia stopped herself and cocked her head to listen.

"Hey, you jerks!" yelled a voice outside the shack. "Come out of there! I've got something to say to you!"

"Is that who I think it is?" Jason asked in disbelief, scrambling to his feet and piling out of the shack with the rest of the group.

"It's Molly!" several of the kids said at once.

Sure enough, standing on an embankment across the tracks some distance away was Molly Lund.

"Who're you calling a jerk?" Hank yelled.

"*All* of you!" Molly yelled back, her voice wafting on a cool, late afternoon breeze. "You're *all* a bunch of losers!"

"You're gonna get it!" Lydia bellowed, storming off toward Molly at a fast clip, with the rest of the group right on her heels.

"Hold on, you guys!" Courtney shouted, skidding to a halt. "Stay away from her! It's some kind of trick!"

Only Jason paid any attention to her. "What do you mean, some kind of trick?" he asked, as the others continued to race toward Molly.

"I'm not sure yet," Courtney replied. "But I know she's setting us up to get even."

"I wonder what she could be planning," Jason said. "I mean, there's seven of us and only one of her."

"All I know is she wants revenge, and somehow she's going to—"

"And you're the biggest jerk of all, Courtney!" Molly yelled, backing away as most of the group came closer.

"That does it!" Courtney exclaimed. "Come on, Jason. Let's get her!"

Fury in her eyes, Courtney raced to catch up to the others, running full tilt and leaping across the train tracks with Jason right behind her. They were scrambling up the embankment to where the others had already surrounded Molly, when suddenly the shriek of a train whistle and the ear-numbing metal-on-metal rumble of a freight train ripped through the air. Stunned, they all watched in terror as sparks flew from the thundering wheels of the racing locomotive as it turned the bend.

Something was clearly wrong with the train, and all of them noticed it immediately. The last car—a boxcar—was lurching from side to side and wobbling crazily. Then there was a loud crack as something snapped and the boxcar abruptly careened off the tracks. Coming apart midair, it flipped over and then plowed into the ground, sending geysers of dust and gravel into the air as it skidded right into the clapboard shack . . . and reduced it to nothing more than a pile of splinters.

"We would have been in there!" Rita gasped, pointing a shaky finger at the spot where the shack had once stood.

"And we would have been killed!" Hank cried, his knees wobbling as he grabbed a spindly tree for support.

Slowly every eye turned to where Molly stood, as the locomotive and the rest of the train squealed to a stop far down the tracks.

"You knew it was going to happen, didn't you?" Lydia asked, her eyes filled with wonder. "You knew there was going to be a train wreck . . . and what would happen if we were in that shack. You knew, didn't you?"

Molly nodded.

"Y-you saved our lives," Courtney stammered in disbelief. "Even after the way we treated you. Why?"

Molly looked from one face to the other, then she turned and began to walk away. After taking only a few steps, she stopped and looked back at the kids. "Tomorrow's going to be a nice day," she said simply. Then she smiled gently and continued on her way.

# Fountain of Horror

ven though Miguel Nuñez and Colby Wilson never expected to actually find the Fountain of Youth, they had a blast year after year tromping around in the Florida Everglades looking for it. Starting ever since they were ten, and going out on their searches mostly on weekends, the two boys often would invite a friend along, and this year they asked Bonnie Finney. Although she was only thirteen—a full year younger than they were—Bonnie had shown so much enthusiasm for their little expeditions that they decided it was OK to invite her along, despite the fact she was a girl. Besides, she was Colby's cousin.

"The legend of the Fountain of Youth started about four hundred years ago," Colby told Bonnie as the three headed out of town on a dirt road that would take them to the swamps. "In Europe and in America there were all kinds of legends about the magical spring. It was believed to be located somewhere here in the Everglades."

"One version of the legend had it that drinking the water would heal all kinds of illnesses," Miguel said, picking up the story. "Other versions had it that the spring gave eternal life or turned old people young."

"Or made people feel happy all the time," Colby added.

"How cool!" Bonnie exclaimed. "I sure hope we find it!" Enjoying playing the role of teacher, Miguel went on. "In 1513 a Spanish explorer named Ponce de Leon led a group of men in search of the fountain."

"Did he ever find it?" Bonnie asked eagerly.

"Not as far as anybody knows," Miguel replied, taking off his cap and mopping his brow, which was damp with perspiration from the hot, early-morning sun. "In fact, nobody knows exactly what happened to Ponce de Leon. According to some historians—"

"Uh-oh," Colby groaned. "Look, Miguel."

Bonnie turned her head in the direction Colby and Miguel were looking. "What's wrong?" she asked.

"It's the Laevich brothers," Miguel whispered.

Up ahead was a run-down store backing onto a large lake, and two smirking teenage boys were lounging on a dock beside the place. A hand-painted sign on the side of the store read: CANAAN CORNERS — BOATS 'N' BAIT.

"Well now, who do we have here?" Wade Laevich, a tall, pimply faced boy, said with a chuckle.

"It's those two fools who are out here looking for the Fountain of Youth year after year," his brother Lyle said, scratching shaggy hair that looked seriously in need of washing. He turned his dull blue eyes on Bonnie. "And it looks like they picked up a *girl* fool, this time!"

"Just leave us alone," Colby warned, taking Bonnie by the arm and quickening his pace.

"Now hold on a second," Lyle said, jumping to his feet and hurrying up behind them. He grabbed Colby's shoulder, then stripped the oversized pack right off the boy's back. "Well, what do we have here?" Lyle asked, as he proceeded to rifle through Colby's and the others' belongings. He tossed a canteen, windbreaker, and compass to the ground but kept the three sack lunches for himself.

Seething, Colby started picking up things from the dirt, and Bonnie and Miguel stooped to help him.

"Hey, now, this is pretty good," Lyle said, already chomping away on one of the sandwiches Miguel's mom had made for the kids. "Nice of y'all to share," he laughed, wiping crumbs from his mouth and then tossing an apple to his brother.

Seeing Colby's face grow red with anger, Miguel leaned in close to his friend. "Just forget these goons," he whispered. "They're not worth it."

"Miguel's right, Colby," Bonnie said. "Let's just go."

"Y'all come back, now, hear?" Wade called, as the three hurried away down the road.

Just then an apple sailed over their heads and splattered against a tree as a resounding belch sounded behind them.

"What pigs!" Bonnie exclaimed, once the three of them were out of earshot.

"You got that right," Miguel agreed, as they headed off the road and down a muddy trail.

"Let's head in a different direction today," Colby suggested, studying his compass. "Let's try due east."

"Sounds good," Miguel said, falling into line behind Bonnie and Colby as they continued plodding through the thickening mud.

Soon they were splashing through ankle-deep water. All around them were towering cypress trees, each covered with Spanish moss hanging limply in the warm, still air like ragged curtains.

"It sure is spooky in here," Bonnie said with a nervous edge to her voice as she gazed around at the dark, shadowy world of the Everglades. The massive cypresses had blotted out huge patches of sunlight and added a gloomy feel to the whole area.

"Spooky but neat," Colby said. "Miguel and I have hiked in here zillions of times, and there's always new stuff to see. I never get tired of the place."

Gradually the footing became firmer, and soon the three kids found themselves scrambling up a grass-covered slope, grabbing hold of vines and reeds for support.

"Hey, what's this?" Miguel asked. He had dropped to his knees, and was wiping dirt off of what appeared to be a round, green-hued piece of metal that was half-buried in the ground. A moment later his eyes grew wide with excitement as he held up a bronze, visored helmet.

"It looks like the kind of helmet the Spanish explorers might have worn!" Colby declared excitedly.

"And what's this?" Bonnie called from a few feet away. She'd been picking through a thick tangle of dead brush and was now tugging on what looked like a big sweater made of knitted metal.

"It's chain mail!" Colby exclaimed. He scurried over and took the moldering piece of body armor from her. "Wow!" he gasped. "It's exactly like something one of the early Spanish explorers would have worn—maybe even Ponce de Leon himself!"

"This is so great!" Miguel cried, stuffing the two prizes into Colby's large backpack. "Come on, let's go look for some more!"

Excitedly the three young explorers hurried over the hill, picking their way over and around boulders down to a broad, slow-moving stream. It took only a moment for them to realize there was something odd about the water. In fact, it was more than odd, it was fantastic. The water was flowing uphill!

"Unbelievable!" the three gasped in awe.

"Let's go!" Miguel cried. "*Vamonos!*"

Scrambling into the weird, up-flowing water, the three splashed up the shallow stream, sometimes plodding along on sandbars that popped up here and there. All the while, a sweet aroma filled the air, and ahead there was the soft, hissing sound of running water. Rounding a bend, they suddenly stopped and gazed spellbound at the sight that greeted their eyes.

"It's incredible!" Colby muttered, staring in amazement.

Before them was a beautiful rainbow cloud out of which poured a pink-hued column of water. It was an upside-down fountain, endlessly taking form in the sky and collapsing downward into a pink-colored pool surrounded by mist.

"This must be the Fountain of Youth!" Miguel cried breathlessly. "We've finally found it!" Without thinking, he dropped to his knees and was about to take a drink when Bonnie grabbed his shoulder.

"Hold on, Miguel," she warned. "We have no idea what's in this water. There could be bacteria . . . or who knows what."

"Bonnie's right," Colby said, taking out his canteen and filling it. "I mean, this probably *is* the Fountain of Youth, but we should take a sample of it back to a lab and have it tested first. Don't you think?"

Miguel reluctantly agreed. "I guess it is better to be careful," he said, a note of disappointment in his voice. "But it sure is tempting. I mean, if this is the Fountain of Youth, then just one drink from it would mean I'd live forever!"

"Let's explore a little farther, then head back," Colby suggested. "Maybe we can find some more old armor or other cool stuff."

Taking a parting look at the beautiful, alluring fountain, the three continued on through the Everglades, slogging in ankle-deep water carpeted with moldering leaves. They made their way along a narrow trail down into a marshy flatland. Overhead the trees formed a vast, living umbrella that completely blocked out the sun, making everything below dark and eerie.

Suddenly Bonnie stopped dead in her tracks. "Look at that!" she exclaimed, pointing ahead.

A few feet away a metal boot was on the surface of the leaf-strewn water. Slowly the three approached it, and as they did they could also see what appeared to be a gauntlet, an armor glove, sticking above the surface.

"Wow!" they shouted in unison as they splashed over to the spot.

But their excitement quickly changed to revulsion. Below, in the shallow water, they could make out a full suit of armor—and inside it was a rotted skeleton.

"Gross!" Miguel said with a groan, peering closer. And then he screamed, and his screams mixed with those of his friends. The gauntleted hand had grabbed hold of his ankle!

"Nooooo!" Miguel cried, kicking free and backing away.

All at once, a man costumed in rusted, corroded chain mail rose from the water. His skin was putrid and slimy, and his eyes, looking like thousand-year-old poached eggs, were transfixed on the three kids. In terror, they back-pedaled as the skeletal man struggled to his feet and reached out his bony arms toward them. "Help me, *por favor!*" the horrid-looking man wailed.

Screaming, the three ran in terror.

"Save me!" the ghastly man cried.

"I think it's one of Ponce de Leon's men!" Colby gasped, as they wildly slogged away through the dark, vile water. "He's still alive! He—"

Suddenly the three stopped abruptly and stood paralyzed with fear. All around them, out of the junglelike gloom, more of the living dead appeared. They rose up from the water, stepped out from dense thickets, and emerged from behind slimy, moss-covered boulders. In Spanish they cried for help . . . and for mercy.

In panic, the kids raced away, stumbling along through the stagnant, stench-filled marsh.

"Which way should we go?" Bonnie gasped.

"Just keep moving!" Miguel yelled.

The footing became firmer, but thick vegetation was now closing in on all sides. They plowed into it, through damp foliage, slapping aside huge, wet leaves and dangling creepers. Then, all of a sudden, a ghastly groaning noise came from somewhere up ahead. The threesome stopped and listened, a cold chill creeping up their spines.

But all had fallen strangely silent.

"This way," Colby whispered, waving them ahead as they made a detour around the area from where the groaning seemed to have come. Miguel and Bonnie nodded and quietly followed. Soon they found themselves entering a small clearing. Numb with exhaustion and fear, the three stopped for a moment and rested.

"Ponce de Leon's men *did* find the Fountain of Youth," Miguel panted, still struggling to catch his breath. "That's who we saw—and they've been living for 400 years. It's horrible—they *can't* die!"

"I just want to get home," Bonnie whimpered, wiping a splatter of mud from her brow. "I'm so scared."

Miguel put a reassuring arm around her as Colby studied his compass.

"Straight north should take us out of here and back to the road," Colby said nervously. "We should be OK, if—"

Colby's mouth dropped open and the hair stood up on the back of his neck. He and his friends grabbed onto each other as another soldier in ancient armor stepped into the clearing. Under his arm . . . was his head!

The mouth of the putrid, flesh-covered skull began to move. "Don't drink the water!" it warned. "Or prepare to live forever!"

"What happened to your head?" Bonnie asked, her face slack with horror.

"I asked one of my companions to kill me, as an act of mercy," the wretched man answered. "But I still live on!"

Colby was almost afraid to ask the next question, but he had to confirm what he already knew to be true. "What is your name, sir?"

"I am Ponce de Leon," the man replied. "Leave this place of evil and never return!"

The kids didn't need to be told twice. Screaming in terror they plowed through greenery, slipping and crawling over tangled roots and rotting trees. Rounding an outcropping of stone, they descended a long slope, then crunched together through a field of dry reeds. Scratched and exhausted, they let out a collective sigh of relief as they broke through the reeds and emerged together onto the road.

"That was so horrible!" Colby cried, with trembling hands wiping leaves and twigs off himself.

For a moment the three paused to catch their breath. They looked back at the dark, frightful swamp, then hurried down the road as fast as their tired legs would take them. Their clothes were torn, wet, and muddy, and they were covered with scratches and bruises, but no one complained, and no one spoke. They were all still too upset and terrified by what they'd just been through.

"Well, if it isn't the great explorers!" Lyle Laevich called as they rounded a bend and approached CANAAN CORNERS BOATS 'N' BAIT. He and his brother were lying in the shade of a huge magnolia tree. "Goodness, they sure are dirty, ain't they, Wade?"

Bonnie, Colby, and Miguel glanced at Lyle and Wade but kept walking, too shaken by their experience to worry about two obnoxious bullies.

"Aren't ya even gonna stop and say hello?" Lyle asked, pretending to be hurt as he and Wade sauntered over.

"Tell us about your explorations," Wade mocked, acting as if he were actually interested. Then, without warning, he stuck his foot out and sent Colby sprawling to the dirt road. In the process, Colby's backpack came loose and out fell some of the things the three had found.

"Hey, now, what's this?" Lyle muttered, picking up the bronze helmet and plunking it down on his head.

"And look at this!" Wade exclaimed, putting on the chain-mail vest and strutting around. Spotting the canteen, he picked it up and shook it. "Why, I do believe I've worked up a powerful thirst," Wade said. Unscrewing the cap, he sniffed the canteen and then poured out some of the water. "It's pink," he mused, "and it smells . . . sweet!"

"Maybe it's cherry soda pop," Lyle suggested.

"Or maybe it's Fountain of Youth water," Wade said with a maniacal giggle. Then without hesitation he brought the canteen to his lips.

"Don't!" all three kids exclaimed in unison.

But their warning went unheeded. "Uhm, that's good!" Wade proclaimed after taking a long swig. He passed the canteen to Lyle, who took several big gulps of the sweet-smelling liquid himself.

Miguel and Bonnie helped Colby to his feet, and then the three exchanged knowing looks, shrugged, and headed off down the road.

"Leaving so soon?" Wade called, the helmet stuck cockeyed on his head. "Oh, well, I guess really important explorers like you have places to go and people to meet. Thanks for everything, y'all!"

Lyle took another swallow from the canteen. "Most generous of you!" he said, looking down and admiring his chain-mail vest.

Colby, Bonnie, and Miguel paused for a moment and looked back at the two bullies.

"Have a nice life," Colby yelled over his shoulder.

"And a long one!" Miguel shouted.

The Laevich brothers just looked at each other in bewilderment. "I wonder what they meant by that," Lyle said, scratching his head.

"Who cares?" Wade said, looking at the three friends who were walking off, leaving the Laevich brothers to their unsavory never-ending future.

# Wax Coffins

White butterflies flapped about like live flower petals, and sunlight filtered through the spruce, ash, and sycamore trees as Linda and her brother Ricky picked their way through woods still damp with early morning dew. Suddenly Linda stopped and touched Ricky's arm. "I have a funny feeling," she said.

"Like what?" Ricky asked. At thirteen, he was a year younger than she, but he always felt like her older brother.

"I feel like we're being watched," Linda replied. "I mean, I'm not even sure it's a person . . . it could be an animal."

Ricky looked around. He noticed a few deer tracks, and high overhead two bluebirds were in a tug-of-war with a worm stretched to its limits between them.

He was about to tell Linda she was imagining things when he happened to notice some bees hovering around a clump of wild honeysuckle some distance away. Squinting through his thick glasses, he realized there was something odd about the bees—he could see them! As far away as they were, and even with his bad eyesight, that meant they had to be unusually large. And what was even weirder, they *did* seem to be watching them.

"Hey, Linda," he began, still looking at the bees. "I think you're right. Take a look at—"

But then he noticed that Linda was no longer by his side. He'd been so engrossed in looking at the bees, he hadn't noticed that she had walked on ahead and was now picking her way down a grassy slope. He hurried to catch up.

"What's that man doing?" Linda asked as her brother stepped up beside her. She was pointing toward a rock-strewn meadow where an elderly man was kneeling over one of many odd-looking wooden boxes. They were all about two feet tall and about a foot wide, except for one that was nearly twice as large. Then her mouth dropped open as she got a better look at the man. His back and arms were completely covered with bees, as though he were wearing a living jacket of the creepy, crawling things!

Seeming to be totally unbothered by the bees, the man's whole attention was on the box before him. From it he had pulled a square panel that was honeycombed with bees.

"Excuse me, sir," Linda called over to him apprehensively. "Are you a beekeeper?"

"That I am," the man replied, barely glancing up.

"I've never seen anything like that," Ricky gasped, his eyes on the writhing swarm of bees. They were now all over the man's bare hands as he handled the square panel. "Aren't you afraid you'll get stung?" he called out.

"Why would they do that?" The man stood up and looked at the two kids without a trace of a smile. "They know I won't hurt them, so why would they hurt me?" He paused for a moment. "Where are you kids from?" he asked, his tone not very friendly.

"We're from Baltimore," Linda replied. "We're visiting our grandparents and other relatives here in Arkansas for spring vacation."

"And we really like it here," Ricky added. "It's beautiful country, and there's—" He stopped himself, realizing that the beekeeper was paying no attention to him at all. Instead, his gaze was fixed on Linda. It wasn't so much that he was looking at her. It was more like he was *thinking* about her.

Then, all of a sudden, the man made an odd clicking noise with his tongue, and the bees on his back and arms took flight. Some settled in the wooden hives while others headed off past an old, run-down house, then continued on into the gaping mouth of a cave up on a rocky hillside.

"How'd you do that?" Linda asked.

"Know anything about bees?" the old man asked her, not responding directly to her question.

"I did a project at school a couple of years ago," Linda said. "I know that there are lots of worker and drone bees, but only one queen. I also know that bees have long, hollow tongues. And the neatest thing is that a bee has five eyes— three small ones in a triangle on its head, and a large compound eye on each side of its head. Each compound eye is made up of thousands of single eyes crowded close together." Feeling proud of all she knew, Linda smiled.

The old man nodded approval. "Do you know how much honey a single bee collects in its lifetime?" he asked.

Both kids shrugged.

"Only one-tenth of a pound—45 grams," the man said almost contemptuously.

"Well," Ricky said with a weak smile, "I guess if that's all they can do, that's all they can do!"

The old man rubbed the stubble of beard on his face. "Well, I say they can do better," he said cryptically.

"Are you working on a way to get them to produce more?" Ricky asked nervously, feeling more and more uncomfortable talking to the man.

An odd smile was the man's only response.

Suddenly a girl's voice called from the run-down house, which was about a hundred feet away. "Thaddius, please come in!" The girl sounded very upset.

Without a word of farewell, the old man headed off to the house with a sour look on his face. A moment later a loud exchange of voices practically exploded from the place.

"Please let me return," the girl in the house pleaded.

"You're too old," the beekeeper snarled. "You've had your five years. Five is the limit!"

Disturbed by the yelling, the kids made a hasty retreat. As they clambered up the bank back into the woods, they heard a door slam and then caught a glimpse of the old man heading up from the house to the cave on the rocky hillside.

"That guy gives me the creeps!" Ricky exclaimed.

"Me too," Linda agreed. "I wonder what he's up to, and who was he arguing with in that house?"

Ricky shrugged. "Well, all I can figure is that he's developing some kind of hybrid bee that will make more honey," he said as they trudged back through the woods. "As far as who that girl was in the house, I—"

Suddenly Ricky cut off what he was saying, and stopped dead in his tracks. There, in neat rows directly in front of them, were several graves. One looked freshly dug.

"There aren't any names on the markers," Linda said, peering closer. "Just initials." Her brow wrinkled. "And look at the birth and death dates. All of these graves are of kids."

"Yeah," Ricky said, shuddering. "And I wonder why this number is written on them?" he asked, pointing below the initials. There, on each of the markers, was the number five.

············

Ricky all but forgot about the whole experience over the next few days, and every time Linda brought it up he told her he wanted no part of returning to where the strange old beekeeper lived. Linda, on the other hand, was consumed with curiosity that would not stop gnawing at her. Finally, one late afternoon three days later, she found her chance to go back and investigate. Her grandparents were going into town to get groceries for the week and later go to a movie. Claiming she wasn't feeling well, Linda told them she was just going to stay home.

"You're going back there, aren't you?" Ricky accused her.

"No I'm not," she lied.

But no sooner had Ricky and their grandparents rattled off down the road in the old pickup than Linda headed off toward the beekeeper's place. Again, as she headed through the woods, she had the feeling she was being watched, seemingly from somewhere high in the trees. And in the far distance she could see what appeared to be a strange flock of birds, almost as though there was a cloud of them darkening the sky. It wasn't until she drew a little closer that her suspicions were confirmed. What she was seeing was a huge swarm of bees.

Knowing that she should be afraid—that she should turn around and run for her life—Linda somehow was compelled to keep walking. She was drawn by a curiosity she couldn't quite explain and by a drive that felt almost like it was inborn.

As she did, she noticed that the flowers in the area were different from what they had been when she and Ricky had passed through a few days before. No longer vibrant and full of fragrance, the wildflowers now were withered and had no scent at all. Even the trees had a dreary, almost lifeless look about them.

"Weird," Linda muttered, feeling once again that she should turn back, but still being driven forward by an overwhelming curiosity.

Entering the meadow where she'd first spotted the beekeeper, she now saw no sign of the man. But there was a bit of smoke wafting from the chimney of the run-down clapboard house, and Linda was certain she'd just caught a glimpse of someone passing by the window.

Feeling a little scared that she might get into trouble for trespassing, she again tried to make herself leave. Instead she found herself walking right up to the house and rapping on the screen door.

"Is—is anybody home?" she stammered, peering through the dark screen that was the only door to the house.

A muffled exclamation came from within, and then

Linda caught sight of a shadowy shape inside the gloomy interior moving hurriedly past.

"Hello!" Linda called a little louder. Then she tentatively opened the screen door and stepped inside.

Gasping, she brought her hand to her mouth to keep from screaming. Standing across the room from her was a shadowy figure.

"Wh-who are you?" Linda asked, squinting into the dim light of the room to make out the shape of a young woman veiled from head to toe in some kind of sheer cloth.

"Leave!" a voice behind the veil ordered. And then, as if pleading, the voice added, "Please, just go!"

"I—I didn't mean to disturb you," Linda stammered, backing toward the door. "Really, I—"

"There's no time to explain!" the voice behind the veil cried. "I don't have long, but you can still save yourself! Run from this horrible place as fast as you can!"

Linda didn't need to be told again. She turned on her heel, bolted from the house, and was soon racing full-speed across the meadow. From behind her, up on the hill, she heard the beekeeper calling after her. But she didn't turn around, or so much as even hesitate. Whatever curiosity had driven her back to this place was now replaced with blind fear that only made her want to get away.

She had almost reached the bank leading up into the woods when a sudden ear-numbing drone filled her ears. It got louder and louder, until Linda felt she would go deaf from the terrible sound. Glancing up, she gazed in terror. Descending on her was a sky-blackening swarm of the largest, most hideous bees she had ever seen. Instantly they were all over her, coating her from head to foot with some kind of sickeningly sweet substance. She screamed in pain and horror as over and over again their stingers pierced her flesh.

...........

Dreamily, her eyes half closed, Linda felt someone lifting her head and feeding her something from a tin cup. It was sticky and sweet like honey, but it tasted, well, glorious!

"Drink," commanded a raspy voice that sounded like that of the beekeeper. "This is my larval nectar. It is the secret of my life's work. Drink this and the last stage of your transformation will be complete."

Unable to help herself—for the liquid was irresistibly good—Linda drank. As though the sweet substance was putting life back into her, she slowly felt energy returning to her body. Now able to force her eyes open, Linda focused on her surroundings and saw that she was in a cave—perhaps the same cave she had noticed before up on the hill. And yes, it was the beekeeper who had been giving her that delicious, energy-building liquid.

"How did I get in here?" she asked, still trying to come back to full consciousness.

Pointing to the beekeeper, the veiled woman stepped out from the shadows. "It was Thaddius—he brought you home," she said. "Just as he brought me here years ago."

A dozen questions were about to tumble from Linda's mouth when suddenly she felt an odd tingling sensation throughout her entire body. Momentarily the sensation became one of intense, unbearable pain . . . as though every part of her being was coming apart.

"The drones did well," the old man said to the veiled woman. "And the larval nectar—" he added, breaking into a maniacal laugh, "—*that*, of course, is the key!"

Then, as suddenly as it had come, the pain vanished, and Linda drifted into a peaceful sleep, with dozens of veiled women bending over her.

...........

Linda felt strange and somehow oddly confined as she again regained consciousness. She opened her eyes and gazed around in disbelief. She was deeper in the cave, it seemed, and the walls of the place were honeycombed. There also was a steady droning that filled the stifling air.

Trying to move, Linda realized that she was standing upright, trapped in a box of some kind. It had a waxy feel to it and had a coffin-shaped design with a thick opaque layer of wax sealing the front of it.

Banging with her fists, she beat on the waxy lid of the box until it began to give a little. Finally it cracked and ruptured slightly. She was screaming for help when first the old man and then the veiled woman came into view, picking their way through the labyrinth of honeycombs that filled the place.

"Help me!" Linda cried. "Get me out of this thing!"

"There is no help for you now," the veiled woman said, "nor for me. My five years are done."

"I don't know what you're talking about!" Linda screamed. "Please—let me out!"

"Our queen's sight seems to be normal," the beekeeper said with a crooked smile. "No more multiple images."

"I'm not a queen!" Linda cried. "What have you done to me?"

"My time is over," the woman repeated, "and yours has just begun." Slowly she raised the long veil, and Linda shrieked in horror, understanding on some primal level that she was seeing a mirror image of herself.

Before Linda stood a mutated being, the face and body a grotesque combination of a young woman and a female bee. Her six limbs were covered with golden fuzz, and each ended in a single, clawlike finger. The compound eyes were made up of hundreds of human eyes. Although her face was that of a teenager, the skin looked wrinkled and sagging, as though in some horrid way it had aged prematurely. The body, too, had a wasted, decrepit look about it.

"I am only sixteen," the poor girl said, a long, hollow tongue flickering in her mouth as she spoke. "But for a bee that is old. The five years of my life are over."

"I don't understand!" Linda wailed, beating so hard on the waxy covering that her hands began to ache. "Why do you keep talking about five years?"

Smiling, the beekeeper made the odd clicking sound Linda had heard before, and suddenly the horrid droning she had noticed moments earlier now resonated throughout the ghastly cavern.

And then the bees swarmed in . . . monster bees the size of footballs.

"Five years is all we live," the transfigured girl said, breathing heavily, her voice sounding like a death rattle. "That is the most we have before we become old and worn out." She smiled wanly. "Then it is time for me to die and a new queen to take my place."

Her face a picture of sheer terror, Linda now saw the gigantic bees crawling all over her wax tomb. They were busily repairing the breaks in the wax that Linda had made by pounding on it with her fists.

"What have you done to me?" Linda cried in horror.

"You are now their queen!" the man said with a maniacal laugh. "It is your turn to reign . . . for five years!"

Linda screamed and screamed. But soon her cries of terror and pleas for help were stifled and all but silenced, as the bees completed their task of sealing her waxy chamber.

# The Electric Girl

Teddy Bennet had been working at his father's law firm, Nash, Rosen & Bennet, for only three weeks that summer when his dad had a heart attack. It had been a scary time for Teddy and his mom, but the doctors had said his dad was going to be fine. They'd given him a pacemaker, an electronic device that would keep his heart beating properly, and told him to take it easy for a few months.

Although his dad had to be out of the office recuperating for a while, Teddy decided to continue working there to keep his mind off his dad. Besides, he wanted to be a lawyer some day, and the job experience would be good.

But the best thing about working at the firm was meeting Mike Jennings, who'd also been hired for the summer. The two fourteen-year-olds had quickly hit it off, and when they found out that they lived close to each other they even started walking to work together.

"I heard they're getting a new secretary today," Mike said one warm morning as they headed into town together. "I heard she's really pretty."

Teddy raised an eyebrow. "Oh?"

"Don't get any ideas, hot-shot," Mike said with a laugh. "She's too old for us. I mean, she's like twenty."

"Yeah, but I'm *so* handsome," Teddy said playfully.

"*You*—handsome?" Mike scoffed as they entered the wood-paneled law firm. "Give me a break!"

In the foyer the two boys helped themselves to a cup of cocoa. Then they set to reshelving dozens of heavy law books in the firm's small library. They were almost done when Mike tapped Teddy on the shoulder and nodded toward the front doorway.

There, surrounded by several law clerks, was one of the prettiest girls Teddy had ever seen. She had long flowing hair and lustrous, shy-looking blue eyes. Her dress was a long, attractive, sort of old-fashioned-looking print.

Teddy took his eyes off the young woman and eased closer to his friend. "You were right," he whispered back. "She's gorgeous."

"Yeah," Mike observed. "Boy, she looks scared."

"Probably just nervous," Teddy said. "After all, this *is* her first day."

Mike grinned. "Well, I guess it's up to—"

Just then Mr. Nash poked his head out of the back room. "As soon as you guys quit staring, could you give me a hand?" he asked. "I have a really 'fun' job for you."

They went into the back room, where Mr. Nash pointed to about a zillion cardboard boxes filled with old papers. "I need you to throw away all the stuff that's not in manila folders," he said, dragging over a recycling container. "Then put all the folders into the file cabinets, alphabetically." He grinned. "I told you it would be fun."

"Hey, we just wish you had more stuff like this for us to do *every* day," Teddy said with a laugh.

To relieve the monotony as they sorted through the tons of old paperwork, the two boys started wadding up papers and shooting baskets at the recycling container. Suddenly they heard someone yell, "Watch out!" from the inner office area. A loud bang followed and then a shattering crash.

Rushing from the back room, Teddy and Mike found a bunch of people standing around the shattered remains of a fluorescent light bulb that had fallen from the ceiling.

"It—it just fell suddenly," one of the clerks stammered.

"Is anybody hurt?" Ms. Rosen, the senior partner, asked.

"Only me," joked one of the secretaries. "I'm going to sue as a result of emotional trauma from the experience."

Surveying the mess, Teddy and Mike didn't need to be told what to do. Teddy got a broom and began sweeping up, while Mike went to the supply closet to get a stepladder and a new light bulb.

They had just finished putting everything back in order when a clerk working the photocopier began grumbling.

"What's wrong with this dumb thing?" she complained. "It just stopped all of a sudden, then started making these weird grinding noises." She bent over and switched the machine off, but a moment later, without anyone touching it, it started up again . . . on its own.

"Totally weird!" Teddy exclaimed.

And then the clerk jumped back. "What's it doing now?"

Everybody nearby was staring at the photocopier. The thing had gone crazy, shooting out papers and sending them fluttering to the floor in a huge mess. Then it broke down completely, spurting photocopier ink everywhere.

Ms. Rosen and the new secretary, Ann-Marie, started picking up papers. Meanwhile, Teddy unplugged the machine and Mike began to mop up the ink. For a moment everything seemed to have returned to normal, until . . .

"I don't believe it!" Ms. Rosen yelled, pointing up at a light fixture in the ceiling.

"What in the world?" Mr. Nash exclaimed, sounding as if he didn't know whether to laugh or be scared.

Looking upward, everyone stared in wonderment as one by one all the fluorescent bulbs began unscrewing themselves, sending everyone diving for cover as the long glass tubes came crashing down.

"This is crazy!" Teddy muttered. He and Mike had taken cover under a desk. "What's going on?"

"Boy, I wish I knew!" Mike answered. "But somebody better find out fast!"

. . . . . . . . . . .

"There's nothing wrong with the lighting system—or the photocopier," the square-shouldered electrician announced. "I've checked everything out, and it seems your circuit breakers are all overloading."

After adding a new ink cartridge to the photocopier, replacing all the fluorescent bulbs, and installing new circuit breakers, the electrician tested everything and left, still unable to provide an explanation as to why it had all happened in the first place.

An hour passed, then two without incident. Everyone was just starting to stop talking about the weird occurrences when suddenly lights all over the office began to flicker on and off.

"Teddy!" Mike called, his voice rising in panic.

Turning around, Teddy saw his friend walking in what seemed like jerky motions through the flickering darkness. Then all at once the strobelike effect stopped and the lights suddenly went back to normal as if nothing had happened. Everybody was standing around gawking and jabbering while Teddy rubbed his eyes in an effort to see normally again. He blinked, then opened his eyes wide. It was then that he noticed Ann-Marie. The new girl was standing across the room with tears coursing down her cheeks.

"You OK?" Teddy asked, going over to her.

Her only response was to shake her head no.

"It was really scary," he said, trying to sound reassuring. "I mean, have you ever seen anything like this before?"

Ann-Marie said nothing, her blue eyes fixed on Teddy in a fearful, unblinking stare.

"What's wrong?" he asked, starting to feel creepy talking to the strangely silent girl.

"I—I have to leave now," she stammered. Then she wiped the tears from her eyes and made her way to the desk where her things were. Instantly, as she approached the desk, the electric typewriter on it began to type all by itself.

Paying no attention to the self-operating typewriter, Ann-Marie quickly gathered up her belongings. "I have to go now," she said again, sounding as though she was talking to herself. Walking stiffly, she headed across the room. As she passed a light switch, it began going wild, flipping on and off by itself. Then a phone rang as she went by, stopping immediately the second she had passed it.

"No!" Ann-Marie cried, sending all the phones into a frenzy of wild rings that wouldn't stop . . . even after people had picked up the receivers.

"It's *her*!" someone yelled out.

Everyone turned and stared at Ann-Marie, and some began to point at the now-trembling girl.

Weeping in earnest, Ann-Marie began to run, sending everything electronic that she passed whirring to life. "Nooo!" she screamed. "Not again!" And with that she raced through the office and disappeared out the door.

Mr. Nash ran after her, but returned only a few moments later. "She's gone," he announced to everyone in the office, which by now seemed to have returned completely to normal. "I followed her down the stairs, but when I got to the lobby only an elderly lady was there. There wasn't a trace of Ann-Marie."

"Why did she run?" Ms. Rosen demanded. "If she had nothing to do with it, she wouldn't have bolted like that."

"Maybe she was just scared," one of the clerks offered.

"Well, I don't know how," a man behind Teddy said. "But I'd be willing to bet that somehow that girl was responsible for all this."

Teddy was about to say that he agreed when, looking down, his eye caught sight of a piece of paper in an electric typewriter. He pulled out the sheet of paper and read what was on it. "Wow," he gasped. He then took another sheet of paper from the print-tray of a word processor, and after that he found a bunch of curled-up sheets from behind the fax machine. On all the pieces of paper the same thing was written: *I have to go now.*

...........

When Mr. Nash asked Teddy and Mike to go on an errand to a different part of the building, the two boys saw the perfect opportunity to do something more fun. On the sly, they checked out Ann-Marie's employee records. Then, within minutes, they were out of the building and headed for the address Ann-Marie had listed. They couldn't wait to find out all about the beautiful young woman with the strange, mysterious powers.

The address was in an area neither boy had been to before. They took several wrong turns, but finally found themselves in front of 3657 Laskin Lane, a huge, fancy house on a secluded tree-lined street.

"Boy, Ann-Marie sure must come from a rich family," Mike commented.

"I'll say," Teddy agreed, as together they made their way up a flower-bordered brick path to the front door. Teddy rapped a heavy brass knocker a few times, waited, then knocked again, louder.

"That's weird," Mike said. "The lights are on."

"Well, maybe they don't want to be disturbed," Teddy suggested. "Ann-Marie was pretty upset, you know."

The two boys had just turned to walk away when out of the corner of his eye Mike saw all the lights in the house suddenly go out . . . all except one.

"Hey, Teddy, check it out," Mike said, pointing to a lighted window on the second floor. It was flashing on and off in the same strobelike way the lights had done in the office earlier that day.

"Let's go see what's up," Teddy said with a mischievous grin, as he pointed to the ivy-covered trellis that went right up to the window. The two walked over and carefully examined the flimsy wooden support.

"I don't think it'll hold both of us," Mike said. "You're lighter. You climb up, and I'll hold the trellis steady."

Teddy started to climb up, hand over hand. "Keep a lookout, OK?" he whispered, looking down at his friend over his shoulder.

Mike gave a thumbs up, and a few minutes later Teddy made it up to the still-flashing window on the second floor. What he saw inside made his blood run cold.

Strapped to an examination table was an ancient-looking woman. She was hooked up to an odd contraption with wires and coils all glowing white with electrical current. Off to the side was an elderly man who appeared to be operating the contraption.

"Are you ready, Ann-Marie?" Teddy heard the voice of the man coming through the slightly ajar window. "I'm going to turn it up."

"I'm ready, brother," the woman replied, a nervous edge to her voice.

Teddy's mouth dropped open at what he saw next. The man threw a switch on the machine hooked up to the woman, and electrical currents surged through her body at a furious rate. As the voltage increased and increased, the elderly woman grew younger and younger . . . until she was completely transformed into the youthful Ann-Marie who Teddy had met earlier that day!

Startled by the amazing event he'd just witnessed, Teddy let out a gasp and at the same moment lost his footing. Mike broke his fall, but the impact left the two boys lying stunned on the ground.

"What did you see?" Mike was finally able to mumble, as he scrambled to his feet and helped Teddy up.

"I'll tell you later," Teddy said. "We've got to get outta—"

"Oh, I don't think you're going anywhere, boys," the elderly man said. He was standing right behind Mike and Teddy. The young Ann-Marie was by his side. "Let me introduce myself. I'm Brendon Thornton, and this is my sister, Ann-Marie."

"But . . . but how . . . ?" Teddy sputtered.

"Ah, now that is a bit complicated to explain," the man said. "However, applying the basic principles of electrical biophysics laid down by such great pioneers as James Watts and Alessandro Volta, I have been able to bring my sister back to life."

"B-back to life?" Mike stammered. "Y-you don't mean Ann-Marie is . . . dead?"

"Not when my brother recharges my neurological system," Ann-Marie said, putting an arm around Brendon. "You see, years ago, when I was only twenty, I drowned in a boating accident. But I was lucky to have a gifted scientist for a brother." She gave Brendon a kiss on his wrinkled cheek. "Actually, Brendon here is my little brother. I know I don't look it, but I'm four years older than he is."

"I haven't perfected the system yet," Brendon said modestly. "As you have seen, Ann-Marie ages rapidly when the 'charge' wears off, and she does have this rather odd effect on electronic devices."

"Wow!" Teddy gasped. "You'd make millions with—"

"No!" Brendon snapped. "You're not to tell anyone! I don't want reporters swarming all over the place. They'll never understand that I created my invention solely for my sister's benefit, and they'll call me a mad scientist."

"But you've got to tell somebody," Mike insisted.

"No one will be telling anyone anything," Ann-Marie said firmly, her soft features turning hard.

"But you're standing in the way of medical science," Teddy pleaded. "You could save millions!"

"Like your father?" Ann-Marie asked.

"What do you know about my dad?" Teddy shot back.

"Now, Ann-Marie," Brendon said tenderly. "The boys aren't going to tell anyone. Your secret will be safe."

"You're not the one they'll call a freak!" Ann-Marie snapped. "You're not the one who needs to be recharged every day. You got used to growing old in the normal way." She smiled bitterly. "I, however, have grown used to being young . . . and you boys aren't going to change that."

"We—we won't tell anybody," Teddy stammered."

Mike nodded vigorously. "Your secret's safe with us."

"Oh, I know it is," Ann-Marie said, her eyes an icy blue. "You see, I overheard your fellow workers today talking about Teddy's father having to wear a pacemaker." The eternally young woman grinned. "You wouldn't want me to drop by for a visit, now, would you, Teddy?"

# Castle of Veins

It was twelve-year-old Lorn Shadduck's first day at Tyler Middle School in Blackwell, Oregon. He was used to going to a lot of different schools—his father was a traveling salesman and the family often had to move with him. Still, Lorn wasn't prepared for how unfriendly most of his new classmates were. Not that they were mean to Lorn, but they did keep to themselves and eyed him with more than the usual suspicion reserved for "the new kid."

Except for Paul Roth. He was the only one who even acknowledged Lorn, and the two boys hit it off immediately.

"How come most of the kids here seem so stuck-up?" Lorn asked as he and Paul poked at gummy-looking macaroni and cheese in the cafeteria. "I mean, I know I'm the new kid and everything, but you're about the only one who's even spoken to me."

Paul pushed a shock of his pitch-black hair off his forehead. "Don't take it personally," he said. "It's just that people in Blackwell are kinda suspicious of newcomers." He shrugged. "I guess you could say that new faces give people in this town the jitters."

"How come?" Lorn asked, washing down the last bite of his cookie with a swig of milk.

"It's kind of hard to explain," Paul replied. "But they're afraid you might not be who you appear to be. They're afraid you might be the freak who lives in the castle—you know, changed into the form of a kid this time."

"Huh?" Lorn grunted. "What castle? What freak?"

Paul laughed. "I guess you haven't heard any of the weird stories going around here."

"No," Lorn said. "I'd have remembered stuff like that!"

"It all started way back in 1904," Paul began. "In that year a castle in Europe was taken apart and then shipped over to America, piece by piece. It was rebuilt in Vanis Woods, not far from town. But nobody knows who had it shipped here or who had it rebuilt. In fact, to this day nobody knows who lives in it."

"You mean somebody *still* lives in it?" Lorn asked, enthralled by the strange tale Paul was telling him.

"Yep," Paul replied. "According to the legend, whoever lived in the castle in 1904 is the same person living there today. You see, whoever it is never ages because it isn't a person . . . it's a vampire!"

Lorn stared in disbelief. "No way!" he gasped. "You're putting me on!"

"Cross my heart and hope to—" Paul began but stopped himself with a sheepish grin. "Well, never mind. Anyway, lots of bodies have been found in the woods with their blood drained, and other people have just disappeared. Some were kids from our school!"

Lorn swallowed hard, unable to speak.

"That's why the weird place built in Vanis Forest is called the *Castle of Veins*," Paul said. "Because of—"

"Gross!" Lorn exclaimed. "So what else do you know about all this?" he asked, his eyes wide.

"Well, our sheriff—and sheriffs before him—have gone to the castle investigating the disappearances, but the owner is never there. They find animals—dogs, cats, rats, and so forth—and sometimes a few strangers hanging around, but no one has actually ever laid eyes on the vampire."

"Why do you suppose that is?" Lorn asked.

"Like I said before, everybody thinks the vampire—or whatever lives in the castle—changes form," Paul replied. "That's how it keeps from being captured, and how it lures victims into the castle to drink their blood." Paul's eyes lit up with excitement as he leaned across the table, closer to Lorn. "Want to hear more about some of the victims?"

Lorn nodded eagerly, his curiosity mounting.

"Around 1921," Paul began, "this woman's daughter was missing, and a few people said they had last seen the little girl going through the gate of the Castle of Veins. So the woman snuck into the place, but she was never seen again. The ironic part is that the little girl had been at her aunt and uncle's house the whole time!"

"So what you're telling me," Lorn said, beginning to understand what Paul was saying, "is that the little girl—"

"Yep," Paul said gravely. "The vampire changed into the little girl to lure her mother into the castle, then it did its vampire number on the mother."

"Wow!" Lorn said breathlessly. "Unbelievable."

"There are tons of stories just as cool as that one," Paul said matter-of-factly. "The most recent one involves a kid who used to go to school here. One morning his dog ran away into Vanis Forest, and the kid went to the Castle of Veins to ask if anyone had seen it. When he got inside the castle, there were *two* dogs that looked exactly like the boy's . . . until one dog changed into the vampire." Paul smiled. "The kid and his dog got away—but the kid's hair turned pure white from fear . . . and so did his dog's!"

"You said this happened in the morning," Lorn commented. "I thought vampires only went out at night."

"Well," Paul said with a shrug, "since nobody knows much about vampires, who really knows *what* they can do? I think people are just guessing when it comes to vampires. I mean, come on," he scoffed, "do you think that a little garlic can scare off a creature as powerful as a vampire?"

Lorn thought for a moment. "Have you ever seen the castle?" he asked.

"Yeah, lots of times," Paul said nonchalantly. "In fact, I'll take you there if you want."

Lorn was taken aback. "I—I," he stammered, trying to think of a good excuse.

"It's not really that far," Paul said, smiling. "We can go there right after school." He arched an eyebrow. "Unless, of course, you're too scared."

"Of course I'm not scared," Lorn said quickly and a little indignantly. "I can't wait to go!"

"Great!" Paul exclaimed, giving Lorn a pat on the back. "I'll meet you by the flagpole in front of the school right after the final bell."

As he watched Paul leave the cafeteria, Lorn shuddered. Boy, what he wouldn't do just to fit in!

...........

The woods were a dark, shadowy, twilight world of tall spruce, fir, and hemlock. It was definitely the perfect place to get a pretty good case of the creeps.

"No wonder people are spooked by this Castle of Veins place," Lorn said, pushing aside long, skinny vines hanging from the surrounding trees like hideous green veins. "This forest itself is scary enough!"

Paul didn't respond.

"Doesn't it kind of get to you, too?" Lorn asked after a moment. "I mean, aren't you just the least bit scared?"

"No," Paul answered. "I guess I'm used to the place."

Lorn wondered what Paul had meant by that, but then decided he was just letting the creepiness of his surroundings affect him. Not wanting to appear frightened, he continued walking behind Paul without comment.

Slowly the two plodded on as the forest seemed to become gloomier and spookier with each step. Soon they entered a swampy area, where the fresh smell of pine was replaced with a pungent odor of mold and decay. And if that wasn't eerie enough, a ground fog now swirled at their ankles and scattered in little puffs with each step they took.

"I thought you said this place wasn't too far," Lorn said. "It seems like we've been hiking forever."

"It's not much farther," Paul answered almost cheerfully. "But if you're getting tired, we could stop and take a rest."

"No, I'm fine," Lorn said, glancing over at Paul, who had an odd look in his eyes.

*He's watching me*, Lorn thought, studying Paul, who now had a smile on his face that somehow looked forced. There was definitely something odd about Paul, but Lorn couldn't quite put his finger on it. Shaking off his suspicions, he continued on in silence.

The trail began to descend sharply, and Lorn soon found himself walking down into a broad, deep ravine. Suddenly the hair stood up on the back of Lorn's neck as a piercing squawk filled the woods and something black flapped by through the trees. Gasping in terror, he jumped as a hand clamped on his shoulder.

"Hey, relax," Paul said with a chuckle. He pointed to where a large black bird was settling down on a branch. "That's just an old crow."

Eyes fixed on the boys, the bird let out another series of ugly-sounding squawks but did not fly away.

"It—it's staring at us," Lorn stammered.

"You look pretty scared," Paul observed. "Want to head back? I mean, I don't want you to end up with white hair, too. You look like you're about to jump out of your skin."

"Me?" Lorn scoffed. "I'm not scared at all. Let's go!"

The stream emptied into a small, dreary-looking lake. They made their way around it, then clambered up a slope with trees clinging precariously to it, their exposed roots looking like tangles of wooden snakes. Reaching the crest, Paul suddenly stopped and pointed.

"There it is!" he announced. "The Castle of Veins!"

Directly ahead was a dark, fearsome-looking structure built on a natural pile of boulders. For a long moment the two boys stared at the foreboding place in awe. Its walls of heavy stone blocks, its large, rounded turrets, and its darkened windows that looked like closed eyes made the place more frightening than either boy had imagined. The drawbridge was open, as though it was extending an invitation to all who might dare to enter.

"Have you ever been inside?" Lorn asked as they crept to within a few dozen yards of the open gateway.

"Inside the Castle of Veins?" Paul asked, his voice a toneless whisper. "Not me! Some kids have bragged that they've gone in there, but they were probably lying."

"I'll bet we could get in and out in a second," Lorn said, trying to sound cool. "Maybe we could even take something—you know, like a souvenir to prove that we've been in there!"

"Well, that *is* sort of a cool idea," Paul replied hesitantly. "We'd be considered the bravest kids in school . . . that is, if we ever make it back to school!"

"Of course we will," Lorn scoffed, feeling more confident as Paul wavered. "*I'm* not scared—are you?"

Paul looked at him and said nothing.

"Of course, you could just stay here," Lorn said, with a smirk, remembering Paul's taunting remarks made earlier, "if you're too chicken to come with me."

Paul frowned, and then a look of determination filled his eyes. "You win," he said, with a wry smile. "We'll both go!"

Sprinting over a grassy patch of open space, then over the hollow-sounding boards of the drawbridge, both boys soon found themselves inside the castle walls. Immediately they began looking around for some sort of souvenir, but found nothing but a bunch of cobwebs.

"Let's get out of here," Paul said. "This place is just a creepy old dump!"

"No," Lorn said. "We have to find something to take. Come on!"

They crept farther inside the enclosed courtyard. From time to time, Paul and Lorn glanced up at the darkened windows, which now seemed to be staring down at them.

"Look!" Paul whispered, pointing at a crumbling old well. He ran over and pried off one of the moldering bricks. "Now we've got proof that we've been here. Let's go."

But Lorn shook his head. "Look, we've come this far. I want to see this vampire with my own eyes."

"Are you crazy?" Paul asked in disbelief. "Isn't seeing the Castle of Veins enough?"

Just then he heard a rumbling, clanking noise. To his horror, Paul saw the drawbridge begin to go up, seemingly on its own.

"Run!" he yelled. But it was too late. The drawbridge closed with a resounding bang.

"We're trapped," Lorn said, in a deathly monotone.

"We can't be," Paul said, desperately turning in circles, looking for some other way out. Then realizing it was useless, he dropped the brick he'd taken from the well. "I guess we won't be needing this anymore," he said, looking helplessly at Lorn. "Now what?"

But Lorn said nothing. His body suddenly was looking very rigid, and his face was now deathly pale, a sickly white . . . as though all the blood had been drained out of it. Woodenly he took a step forward.

"Lorn, we've got to find a way out!" Paul exclaimed. "Pull yourself together, man!"

"There is no way out," Lorn said, his voice a barely audible whisper.

"There's got to be!" Paul insisted.

"You should have listened to the warnings about this place," Lorn said. "You were right to fear newcomers. You never know who they *really* are, do you?"

Paul gazed in horror. He loved scaring new kids with tales of the castle, but he never actually believed any of them . . . until now.

"I have always found it fascinating how gullible the young are," Lorn said, his voice growing deeper.

Then all at once Lorn's face lengthened and his bones crackled as his body grew into that of a towering, cloaked being, with eyes black as coal—and fathomless.

"Nooooo!" Paul cried.

"Oh, yes," the creature said with an evil smile. "I can't tell you how many times I've used this new-kid disguise as bait. It's harder to get kids to follow you since they like to snub newcomers, but I like the challenge of finding that one 'nice' kid who'll make a very *nice* meal!"

And with that, the hideous vampire let a hiss escape him as his mouth opened wide, exposing razor-sharp fangs.

Paul screamed, then fell silent, as the thing that had once been just "the new kid" satisfied its terrible hunger.

# Brain Pictures

**F**ifteen-year-old Jenna Paisley's eyes were riveted on the book she was reading. "Awesome!" she exclaimed. She was slouched on her brother Jerry's bed.

"What?" Jerry asked, looking over his shoulder. An avid model airplane buff, he was sitting at his desk working on a B-29, a bomber airplane used during World War II.

"This book I'm reading," she replied. "It's about people with weird powers."

"You mean things like ESP and all that other goofy psychic stuff you think you've got?" Jerry asked.

Jenna rolled her eyes. "No, the part I'm reading now is about a man named Ted Serios," she replied. "Back in the sixties, he took photographs of things in his mind."

"Yeah, right!" Jerry scoffed.

"It's for real," Jenna insisted. "Listen, I'll read what it says. 'Surrounded by at least a dozen witnesses, Ted Serios of Chicago repeatedly aimed an instant-picture camera directly into his eye. When he saw something passing through his mind, he snapped a picture. Among the brain pictures that Serios took were an image of the White House's dome and the Queen of England.

" 'Conducting scientifically controlled experiments performed inside a solid steel chamber,' " Jenna read on, " 'scientists themselves took many of the photographs, and would not even allow Serios to touch the camera. In fact, twenty-five scientists signed statements that the tests could not have been faked and that Serios actually had been photographing his own thoughts.'"

"Well, it still sounds pretty hokey to me," Jerry said.

"Know what?" Jenna exclaimed, jumping up from the bed and heading out of the room. "I'm gonna try it. I'm gonna take pictures of the stuff in *my* brain!"

"Won't work," Jerry called, following her into the family room. "There's nothing in your brain!" He found Jenna rummaging through a closet, and when she turned around, she was holding an old instant-picture camera.

"Good," she said, checking to see if there was any film in it. "It's still got nine shots left." Then, with Jerry shaking his head as he watched her, she sat down on the couch and looked straight into the lens with her right eye. "Well, here goes nothing," she said, and opening her eye as wide as she could, she clicked the shutter.

Instantly the camera made a whining mechanical noise, and a moment later a picture emerged.

"Weird," Jerry said, taking the self-developed print his sister handed him. "It looks like a close-up of my face. You must have turned the camera around really fast when I wasn't looking."

"You know I didn't," Jenna replied. "You were right here watching me the whole time." She ran a hand through her hair, deep in thought. "And it *does* make sense, Jerry. I mean, think about it—your face was the last thing I saw before I snapped the picture."

"Try doing it again," Jerry suggested, now genuinely intrigued by his sister's strange experiment. "Maybe there was something to that weird Serios guy."

Again Jenna aimed the camera. She closed her eyes waiting for an image to pass through her mind, then she suddenly opened her eyes and clicked off a picture. When it came out of the camera, the two found themselves looking at a photograph of a springer spaniel.

"It's Ruffy!" Jerry blurted. "And he's in our backyard."

"This is so cool!" Jenna cried with excitement. "I was thinking about Ruffy! I saw him in my mind, playing in the backyard just the way he used to!"

After staring at the picture of their dog that had died several years ago, Jerry took a couple of turns trying to take pictures of his mind. Nothing came out but blurs.

"I wonder why it works for you and not for me," he said, frowning as he handed the camera back to his sister.

"To be honest," Jenna said, "I don't know why I—"

Suddenly a faraway look came into her eyes. She quickly raised the camera and snapped a picture. Only the whirring sound made by the camera as the photograph came out seemed to jar Jenna out of her trance.

"Who is that?" Jerry asked as he examined the photo and then handed it back to his sister. It was a picture of a little boy with neatly combed hair that looked like it had pieces of white confetti in it. He was holding a carton of some kind.

"I never saw him before in my life," Jenna said. "In fact, I don't even remember what I was thinking about when I took the shot." She studied the picture for a moment, then tossed it aside with a shrug. She was just raising the camera to eye level to take another shot when the doorbell rang.

With a groan, annoyed at being interrupted, Jenna got up and opened the front door. An icy winter breeze wafted into the house, but it wasn't the cold that sent a chill down Jenna's spine.

A little boy with white flecks of snow in his neatly combed hair was looking up at her . . . and he was holding a carton of some kind. "Hi, my name is Chad Ellis," he said. "And I'm selling candy to raise money for our soccer team."

Jenna stared in disbelief. It was the same little boy in the picture she'd taken moments before—*in her mind!*

Seeing the shocked expression on Jenna's face, the boy stepped back. "Y-you OK?" he stammered.

"No, I'm not," Jenna mumbled. "And I don't want any candy." She quickly shut the door. "Jerry! You won't believe what just happened!" Jenna yelled at the top of her lungs as she raced back to the family room.

...........

After telling Jerry about the little boy, Jenna sat on the edge of the sofa, still shaken. Jerry immediately wanted her to take more pictures, but she was reluctant. What had just happened had left her feeling disturbed and very jittery.

"Don't you get it?" she asked, her voice trembling. "The picture was of somebody I'd never seen before!"

"Well, you've always said you have premonitions and stuff," Jerry said with a shrug. "Maybe you *do* have ESP."

"I admit that sometimes I get feelings that something is going to happen," Jenna replied. "But I've never seen them in my head—let alone taken pictures of them!"

"So you're telling me that before that kid came to the door you never saw him in your head?" Jerry asked. "He never crossed your mind even once?"

"No. That's what I've been trying to tell you!" Jenna said, getting a little frustrated. "The premonition was there, but I didn't know what it was until I'd photographed it."

Jerry handed her the camera. "Come on, Jenna. Take some more pictures. I mean, this is just too cool to stop doing it now."

Jenna was about to say no when suddenly a strange, eerie feeling swept over her. She quickly put the lens to her eye, and then, like a person possessed, she took one shot after another, not even bothering to see what was coming out. Not until she was out of film did she finally stop.

After all the prints had developed, the two kids laid them out on the floor and studied them.

"Weird," Jerry said in a hushed tone.

There was a picture of their mom's favorite necklace tangled in a shrub. And there was one of an ordinary telephone, seemingly the one in the family room, but with something spilled on it. The next shot was of the back door of their house, and it was opened onto the backyard. And the last one was of a hooded, dark blue jacket with red cuffs.

"I don't know what to make of all this," Jenna said, scanning the pictures.

Suddenly the two kids jumped when a door slammed.

"Helllooo!" their mom called. "We're home!"

Jenna pushed the camera and pictures behind the sofa, then she and Jerry hurried out to greet their parents. "I know we're late," their mom said. "Hope you guys weren't worried, but they had a big sale over at Sports World, and your dad and I decided to check it out."

Their dad smiled and reached into a big shopping bag. "Sorry I couldn't find anything in your size, Jenna," he said. Then he turned to Jerry. "But we did find something for you, sport." He pulled a nylon jacket from the bag. "I know you like to wear things oversized, so we got you a large."

"Uh, thanks," Jerry said, looking at the jacket and swallowing back a wave of fear. The jacket was dark blue, hooded, and had red cuffs.

...........

Jenna and Jerry were too freaked out to tell their parents about Jenna's mind pictures. Besides, right after dinner, their mom and dad took off for their workouts at the gym, so there wasn't time to get into it anyway.

"Let's go to the drugstore and buy some more film," Jerry said excitedly as soon as their parents had left.

As curious as her brother, Jenna agreed, and the two hurried to the corner drugstore through fleecy, drifting snow. When they returned, they made some cocoa to warm up, then headed into the family room where they began to take more pictures of the images in Jenna's mind.

The first two pictures were scary. One showed a man with a pockmarked face and thick eyebrows, and the other was a close-up of an outstretched hand—with only three fingers. The picture of the three-fingered hand gave them the creeps, but the next one completely horrified them. It was a picture of Jerry, in his new jacket, lying facedown in a pool of blood on the back walkway.

Jerry looked down at his new jacket, which he had been wearing ever since they had gone to the drugstore. "I'm taking this off!" he announced, then put down the last photo on the end table next to the sofa. "I'm afraid to even look at this last picture," he said with a shudder.

Jenna was reaching for the photo and Jerry was starting to unbutton his jacket, when suddenly both kids froze and their eyes went wide as saucers. From a back room came the tinkle of breaking glass . . . then the sound of footsteps.

"Somebody's in the house!" Jerry whispered. Then turning abruptly, he bumped into Jenna, knocking the cup of cocoa in her hand and splashing it all over the phone.

"We have to stay calm," Jenna whispered back.

Hair standing up on the back of their necks, the two listened as floorboards creaked in the hallway. Then they heard the clinking of silver in the dining room.

"We're being robbed!" Jerry whispered. "I'm going to take a look. You duck behind the sofa."

Tiptoeing to the door, Jerry peeked down the hallway.

"Hey, punk!" snarled a voice.

From her hiding place behind the sofa, Jenna saw her brother being pulled out into the hall by a man . . . with bushy eyebrows and a pockmarked face!

"Is anyone else in the house?" the man demanded.

"N-no, nobody else is here," Jerry gasped, his voice reduced to a hoarse rasp by a stranglehold on his neck.

"You better not be lying, punk," the man growled. "Now lead the way to where your parents keep their good stuff!"

Still hiding, Jenna heard receding voices and footsteps that seemed to be headed toward her parents' bedroom. Trying to figure out what to do, she scanned the room for a weapon, and her eyes fell on the phone across the room. It was still drenched in the cocoa Jerry had caused her to spill.

All at once a dark thought hit her—that was one of the pictures she'd taken! What if the other photographs she'd taken came true as well? In her mind's eye she could see the picture that terrified her most, the one of Jerry lying on the back walkway . . . in a pool of his own blood.

"I've *got* to get to that phone!" she whimpered, growing more upset by the moment. "I've got to call the police!"

Taking a deep breath, Jenna began to ease out from her hiding place. She had almost reached the phone when suddenly from another room came the sound of a scuffle. There was a yell of anger from Jerry, quickly followed by a loud *thunk*. Then heavy footfalls sounded in the house. Cautiously Jenna made her way from the family room, and as she did, she caught a glimpse of her brother hurrying out the back door—after the burglar!

"No! Jerry!" she screamed, running through the house. "Just let him go!"

But she was too late. From outside there was a yelp followed by a sickening *thud*.

"Jerry!" Jenna cried, hurrying out the back door and into ice-cold air . . . where she stopped and stared in horror. There, still wearing his new jacket, was Jerry in the same position as he'd been in the photograph—facedown in his own blood.

"No!" she sobbed as she knelt down and turned him over . . . but it wasn't Jerry! Instead, lying unconscious in a growing pool of his own blood, was the man with the pockmarked face.

Confused, Jenna looked around, and saw a green trash bag lying open in the snow right next to a shrub with her mom's favorite necklace tangled in the branches. Then suddenly, from inside the house, she heard Jerry yelling to her, his voice oddly muffled.

Hurrying into the house, she found her brother lying on his side in a hallway. His hands were tied and there was a gag in his mouth . . . and he wasn't wearing his jacket.

Right away, Jenna realized what had happened. The burglar had stolen Jerry's new oversized jacket—along with everything else—then had slipped on the ice and knocked himself out while fleeing out the back door.

"Hang on, Jerry," Jenna said to her brother, whose eyes were wide, as he struggled to say something to her. "I'll have this gag off in a minute." She was still working on the gag when Jenna suddenly heard the burglar groaning outside. "Oh, no!" she cried. "He's starting to come to!"

Leaving Jerry's gag still partially tied, she raced off. "I'll be right back!" she called over her shoulder to her still-struggling brother. "I've got to call the police before that guy regains consciousness and gets away!"

"Jenna!" Jerry yelled, his voice still muffled by the gag.

"Hold on!" Jenna called as she quickly punched in 911.

Within seconds, Jenna had the police dispatcher on the line and was nervously describing what had happened. As she spoke, her eyes fell to the photos she'd taken earlier. They were still lying scattered on the end table.

"Jenna!" Jerry yelled, his voice clear now that he'd managed to work the gag out of his mouth. "Jenna, get out of the house!"

"A squad car is on its way," the police dispatcher was saying. "Please stay on the line."

But Jenna was too petrified to answer. Her gaze was fixed on the last photograph, the one she hadn't seen . . . until now. It was a picture of herself . . . lying on her back on the floor, her own dead, glazed eyes staring sightlessly back at her.

"There were *two* burglars—and the other one is still in the house!" Jerry screamed.

Horrified, Jenna heard a creak behind her. Slowly, stiffly, almost robotically, she turned around . . . as a three-fingered hand suddenly closed over her mouth.

# Horror in Room 519

Brian Tyler's older sister, Jenny, had warned him about Mr. Zimmer's science class. When Jenny had gone to Cascade Middle School two years ago, she had to endure the tough, grumpy old science teacher. Now it was Brian's turn—only he had to endure the grouch starting with first period.

"What a way to start the day," Brian muttered under his breath as he stood before room 519, the science lab. "Well, others have made it through Zimmer's class, and so will I."

Taking a deep breath, he walked into the room. But instead of the wizened old professor he thought he'd find, Brian was surprised to see a young woman at the podium. She was rustling through a bunch of papers and glancing nervously from the clock to the kids who were now taking their seats.

"Where's Mr. Zimmer?" Brian whispered, sitting down in a front-row seat next to Dirk Roxbury, his next-door neighbor and one of his best friends.

"Didn't you hear?" Dirk whispered back. "Zimmer died at the beginning of summer vacation." He motioned with his head toward the young woman who appeared young enough to still be in college. "Looks like we lucked out."

"Yeah, but it's too bad we still have to take science," Brian said, looking around the room. "All the stuff in here gives me the creeps."

Brian shuddered. Hanging on a pole just a few feet away was a human skeleton. On the counter, next to a fat gopher snake slithering around in a large aquarium, were beakers, test tubes, and big jars of formaldehyde. There were all kinds of gross things floating in those jars, and Brian was pretty sure several of them contained animal organs. One of them actually held a brain!

"If anyone makes me touch animal guts, I'm gonna puke!" he said to Dirk.

His friend chuckled. "I like science. I mean, look at all the cool stuff we get to mess with." He gestured toward two glass cabinets filled with all sorts of scientific equipment.

"I don't know," Brian replied, looking at dozens of thick, brand-new books that filled an entire wall of shelves. "It looks to me like it's going to be a tough class—even *without* old man Zimmer teaching it."

Just then the starting bell rang—and the teacher just about jumped out of her skin. "Hello, class," she said, her voice cracking. "I-I'm Ms. Gytry, and I'll be taking Mr.

Zimmer's place. As you may have h-heard," she stammered, "Mr. Zimmer passed away recently. He was a wonderful teacher, I've been told, and I'll do my very best to measure up to his high standards." She forced a stiff, self-conscious smile, and then went about taking attendance.

"Boy, she looks scared to death," Brian said, elbowing Dirk and snickering under his breath.

"Yeah, I wonder what she's so nervous about," whispered Colette Rey, a red-haired, green-eyed girl sitting behind Brian and Dirk.

"Got me, C-C-Colette," Mike Barnes said just after Ms. Gytry stuttered out his name. "But I got a hunch this class is g-gonna be a t-trip."

"Stop making fun of her, Mike," Gina Adams scolded. "She's just a little uptight. We should all give her a break. This is probably her first time teaching."

Frank Lopez tapped Mike gently on the arm. "Gina's right," he said. "Let's go easy on her."

"N-no talking back there, please," Ms. Gytry said weakly. Then, as though gathering up every ounce of courage she had, the trembling teacher began walking around the classroom, passing out a piece of paper to each student. "This is your class outline," she said, her voice gaining confidence. "Make sure you keep it in your notebooks. It covers our entire—" Suddenly she let out a little yelp as her foot caught on something and she stumbled. The stack of papers went flying from her hands.

"How clumsy of me!" Ms. Gytry cried, her face turning red as she began picking up papers with a few students who had bent down to help her.

"Could happen to anybody, Ms. *Jittery!*" a boy called out.

As the entire class burst into laughter, Brian turned to Mike. "Like you said, Mike," Brian whispered, "this class is gonna be a trip!"

...........

It was pretty obvious from that first day that Ms. Gytry was in for a pretty horrific semester. But it wasn't until the third day of class that the novice teacher fell victim to her students' first major attack.

"Oh, no!" Ms. Gytry gasped the moment she walked into room 519. Her eyes blinked in disbelief as she looked from one disaster to another. Beakers and test tubes were glued to the ceiling. The frogs had been set free from their plastic containers and were now hopping around the room. And weirdest of all—a cow liver had been removed from its formaldehyde solution and was now in the fish tank.

"How terrible!" Ms. Gytry exclaimed.

"Yes, it *is* terrible," Mike said with a straight face. "Who could have done such an awful thing?"

"We'll help you clean up the mess, Ms. Gytry," Colette said, her face a mask of innocence. "Come on, guys," she said to her classmates. "Let's give Ms. Gytry a hand."

Brian, Mike, Colette, and Dirk—along with half a dozen other kids—were behind the whole thing, and everybody in class knew it. But nobody said anything. Instead, everybody just went to work, and soon they had the room cleaned up.

When they were done, Ms. Gytry, who was now quite angry, gave the class an assignment from their text that was obviously just busy work so she could collect herself. Then right before the final bell, she took the podium.

"I suppose some of you think this was funny," she said, her voice quavering a bit. "But it was an awful thing to do. You may not be aware of it, but many of the things in this room—many of which were destroyed—were donated to the class by Mr. Zimmer. He loved teaching, and he loved this room. He taught here for over forty years, and it was his dying wish to leave as much as he could to his students."

"Gee, what a dedicated guy," Dirk said with a smirk.

"I know that Mr. Zimmer had a reputation for being strict," Ms. Gytry went on, ignoring Dirk's comment. "But I got to meet him before he passed on, and he really was a very caring person with a marvelous sense of humor."

"Yeah, I'll bet he was a real barrel of laughs," Brian whispered to Dirk.

"I heard he never cracked a smile in his entire life," Dirk replied with a laugh.

"You two stop talking back there!" Ms. Gytry demanded.

"Sorry, Ms. Gytry," Dirk said with mock sincerity.

Brian folded his hands on his desk and smiled innocently. "Won't happen again," he lied, as he quietly began cooking up a new and even better prank.

...........

When Ms. Gytry came into class on the following Monday morning, she was deep in thought about magnetism, the lesson for the day. She'd spent a lot of time making the subject as interesting as possible, and she hoped the kids would like it—at least enough to behave themselves.

"Good morning, everybody," she said with a smile, delighted to see all her students already seated.

Wondering what everyone was grinning about, Ms. Gytry plunked her tote bag on her desk. Then she pulled open the top drawer to get the roll book . . . and let out a shriek that reverberated throughout the room.

Instantly the class burst into laughter. Then, after seeing tears leap to Ms. Gytry's eyes as she retrieved Henry, the gopher snake, from her desk, they quickly quieted down.

"I don't know why you're so cruel," she said, struggling to keep her composure. "I guess you think it's funny. But now that you've had your big laugh for the day—" Suddenly she stopped herself and stared at the ordinarily vacant seat in the back of the room. There, sitting upright, wearing a jacket and a cap on its head, was the class skeleton. A notebook was open in front of it and a pencil was clutched in its bony fingers.

"How dare you make a mockery of this class!" Ms. Gytry yelled as she stomped over to the skeleton and snatched the pencil out of its hand. Then after removing the cap and jacket, she returned the skeleton to its stand. "You don't even realize what a despicable thing you've done!" she shouted. "This skeleton—like all the new books and practically all the equipment in this room—was a donation from Mr. Zimmer. If I were him I'd be turning in my—" All at once, Ms Gytry stopped midsentence. Unable to go on, she simply sat at her desk and burst into tears.

. . . . . . . . . . .

"Maybe we went too far today," Colette said to Brian, Mike, and Dirk later that afternoon. The four kids who were primarily responsible for putting the snake into Ms. Gytry's drawer and dressing up the skeleton were over at Brian's house. They often met there to shoot some hoops, but today they were sitting in Brian's room, not feeling like doing much of anything.

"Did you hear that shriek she unloaded when she saw Henry?" Brian asked. "She practically broke my ear drums."

"It was awesome!" Mike exclaimed. "And the skeleton bit was—"

"But she cried!" Colette interrupted. "I didn't expect *that*! I mean, I kinda felt sorry for her."

"Oh, come on," Dirk scoffed. "If Ms. *Jittery* can't take a joke, that's *her* problem."

"The way I see it," Mike said with a crooked grin, "we're doing her a favor. New teachers gotta learn the ropes, and it's up to us to help her out—you know, toughen her up."

Colette shrugged. "I don't know," she said. "I still think maybe we should lay off her—at least for a while."

"Nah," Brian said. "The real fun hasn't even started!"

...........

The "real fun," as Brian had put it, began three days later when the class skeleton disappeared altogether. It wasn't seated at a desk or hidden somewhere in the room. It was just plain gone.

Ms. Gytry, trying to maintain her cool, calmly went around the room and asked each student if he or she knew where the skeleton was. But when no one would admit they'd taken it or knew where it was, she curtly said, "Fine," assigned them all extra homework, then began conducting the class as if nothing had happened.

At lunch everyone was buzzing about the missing skeleton. Theories about its whereabouts flew around the lunchroom, and one kid even suggested that it ended up in the cafeteria's "special of the day." No one, however, would admit taking it.

"Ms. Jittery probably got rid of it so we couldn't pull any more stunts with it," Brian suggested to the others. "Either that or old man Zimmer came back from the grave to reclaim his bones!"

Everyone laughed, and the conversation slowly changed to other subjects. But as the others jabbered away, Brian kept thinking about the missing skeleton. What *had* happened to it, he wondered. And why didn't *he* think of taking it first?

...........

That night Brian's parents went to his sister's school play, which Brian got out of by claiming he had too much homework to do. But as soon as his parents drove off, instead of hitting the books, Brian got ready to go next door to Dirk's house—as planned—and kick back with Dirk and some of their other friends.

Grabbing his wallet off his dresser, Brian then went to his closet to get his jacket. Hardly paying any attention, he opened the door . . . then screamed at the top of his lungs.

Standing in the closet grinning at him was the skeleton!

Tearing out of his room, Brian made a mad dash to the phone in his parents' room to call Dirk.

"No way!" Dirk exclaimed once Brian told him what was in his closet. "Listen, Mike is already here with me. We'll be right over!"

Terrified, his hands trembling, Brian hung up. Someone was playing one heck of a trick on him. But who? Sitting on the edge of his parents' bed and trying to calm down, Brian's eyes suddenly went wide with horror. Was it his imagination or had someone—or something—just walked by outside his parents' bedroom? His heart racing, Brian stepped into the hall . . . and heard the back door of the kitchen softly close.

At almost the same instant the front doorbell rang.

He crept into the front hallway. Reaching the door, he put his ear up against it and stammered, "W-who is it?"

"It's Dirk and Mike, you jerk!" he heard two familiar voices yell in unison.

With a sigh of relief, Brian let in his friends, and talking a mile a minute, he led them to his room. "Take a look," he said, pointing to the opened closet door.

"At what?" Dirk asked.

Brian stared into the closet. But there was nothing in it except a bunch of clothes.

"Oh, I get it!" Mike said with a laugh. "You were putting us on!"

"No," Brian said. "There was a skeleton in there—I swear it! And when I was calling you, I heard somebody sneaking out of the house!"

"Maybe it was Ms. Gytry," Dirk suggested. "Maybe she figured out it was your idea to mess with the skeleton in the first place, and she just wanted to get even with you."

"Nah," Mike said. "A teacher would get fired for a stunt like that."

"Well, *somebody's* trying to freak me out," Brian exclaimed. "And if I find out who's doing—"

Mike's eyes lit up. "You know, Brian," he said excitedly, "I'll bet whoever pulled this number on you is taking Mr. Bones back to school—right this second!"

Without another word, the boys were out the door heading for the school, and in less than fifteen minutes they were sneaking through the same basement window with the bent latch they'd gone through to pull their last couple of pranks. Soon after that, Brian, with a boost from his two friends, was crawling through room 519's transom, and a moment later he'd opened the door to let in Dirk and Mike.

With their nerves on edge, the three boys looked around the dark, eerie classroom. All was silent and creepy. Mike was pointing to the empty stand where the skeleton had been, when suddenly they heard the sound of footsteps.

"Someone's coming!" Dirk whispered, as the four scrambled behind a lab counter and hid.

The footsteps came closer and closer, and then someone entered the room. From their hiding place the boys could hear the sound of chalk scraping on the blackboard. Their hair standing on end, they peeked over the counter and saw who or *what* was writing on the board.

Screaming in horror, they bolted from the room, raced down the hall, burst through the school's front doors and tore down the street—not stopping to see the bony hand that waved at them from the window in room 519.

· · · · · · · · · · ·

The next morning in class, Ms. Gytry was surprised and pleased by the message on the blackboard. *Everyone is going to treat you with the respect you deserve from now on*, it read.

And she was delighted to see the skeleton once again hanging from its stand.

"I can't tell you how relieved I am," she said happily. "You see, this was not just an ordinary skeleton. Before Mr. Zimmer passed away, he donated many things to the school . . . including his *own* skeleton. It was his final wish to forever remain in this classroom, as he said in his last will and testament, 'to guard over room 519 forever.'" She shook her head and smiled. "You know, all teachers should have the dedication Mr. Zimmer had."

Brian, Dirk, and Mike shuddered, then looked at each other and nodded. Only they knew just *how* dedicated Mr. Zimmer really was.

# Return from Nowhere

A mber Andersen and her parents were in a good mood as they checked into the motor lodge in Doncella, New Mexico. As the travel agent had promised, the lodge was beautiful. And the town of Doncella itself, with its Spanish architecture and tree-lined streets, was even prettier than it had looked in the brochure.

But the Andersen family knew nothing of the bizarre history of Doncella. And they had never heard of one of its most infamous residents, Jeremy Tate. All they could gather from the town gossip was that the man had returned, and everyone in town was pretty weirded out by it.

When Jeremy had appeared two days ago dressed in outdated clothes and looking very confused, people had scuttled away in fear. Some had taken pictures of him on the sly and then hurried away. At the town's expense, he had been put up at a local hotel so people could keep an eye on him. And townspeople stood in the street and gawked up at the window of the second-story room where he was staying, still amazed that he had come back.

For although Jeremy Tate looked like a man of twenty-nine, which was how old he'd been when he had literally disappeared off the face of the earth, he was now well over one hundred years old. You see, no one had laid eyes on Jeremy since 1885.

It seemed that everybody in Doncella except Amber and her parents knew the story of Jeremy Tate. They heard bits and pieces, but not until they picked up the local newspaper did they begin to understand what all the fuss was about.

"What does it say about him, Mom?" Amber asked eagerly after they had returned to their motel room with a copy of the newspaper. Mrs. Andersen sat down on the bed, pushed her bifocals higher onto the bridge of her nose, cleared her throat, and started to read.

"'It was the morning of November 11, 1885. On a ranch, seven miles from Doncella, New Mexico, Jeremy Tate, 29, and Margaret, his wife, 28, sat on the front porch of their adobe ranch house, watching their two children, Rachel and Stuart, play in the front yard. After a while, Jeremy spotted two people driving toward the farm in a buggy. He waved and headed across an open field to greet his guests, who turned out to be Mayor Leonard Hudd and his daughter, Judith. As he approached them, Jeremy suddenly stopped, looked back at his family, then back across the field. The mayor shouted hello. And that's when it happened—Jeremy

Tate vanished into thin air. One minute he was standing in an open field, and the next minute he was simply gone.'"

Amber's mom put down the paper. "That's amazing!"

"It's not just amazing," Amber said, "it's impossible."

Amber's dad leaned over his wife's shoulder and looked at the article. "Keep reading," he said. "This is fascinating."

"'Mrs. Tate and the two men went to the spot where Tate had disappeared, certain that he fallen into a gully or crack in the earth,'" Amber's mom read on. "'But they found nothing. Neighbors from far and wide came to the Tate farm to search the field, but there was still no sign of Jeremy. Finally a geologist was called in to examine the land, and he found nothing but limestone bedrock. There were no fractures or cavities in the ground whatsoever.'"

"How weird!" Amber gasped. "The guy just vanished like a magician—*poof!*"

Her mother nodded. "It certainly is weird. And listen to this: 'The following spring, the grass where Tate had disappeared had grown high and thick in a perfect circle, fifty feet in diameter. Cattle and other farm animals would not go near the place, and it even seemed free of insects.

"'One day in July 1886, Tate's two children reportedly approached the circle of high grass. They called out for their father several times and suddenly heard a faint cry for help, but they couldn't tell from where. Excited that they might have found their father, the two children raced off to the house and returned with their mother to the exact same spot in the field. She supposedly heard her husband calling her name, but Jeremy Tate himself never reappeared.'"

"Not until two days ago," Amber's father scoffed, rolling his eyes. "If you ask me, this fellow claiming to be Tate is using a local folk tale to fool everybody. He's already gotten a free room at the hotel. Now he's probably looking to get a book deal out of it."

"Yeah," Amber said with a chuckle. "He'll probably claim he went into a different dimension or was picked up by a UFO or something."

"Well, this article says that the man who recently walked into town claiming to be Jeremy Tate supposedly doesn't remember any part of the incident," her mother said. "According to him, all he remembers is watching his kids play one minute, then walking into town the next."

"I still don't buy it," Amber's dad said skeptically. "I think this guy is nothing but a fraud."

"Well, if that's true, he's a fraud on the verge of a nervous breakdown," Amber's mom replied. "When I went to the ATM this morning I heard people saying that Mr. Tate is really distressed and totally baffled by what's happened to him—or should I say, by what people *say* happened to him. All he wants is to be with his wife and kids, not to mention his friends. Everyone he knew back in 1885 has long since passed away."

Amber walked over to the window and looked at the hotel where Jeremy Tate was staying, just down the block. "Poor guy," she said thoughtfully. "If he *is* telling the truth—which seems impossible—he's sure going to be lonely, what with everyone in town thinking he's a liar or nuts."

"Well, I say the guy just looks like Tate and is trying to cash in on it," Amber's dad insisted. "I mean, there's no way someone can be missing for as long as Tate has without aging a single day. I wouldn't believe a word of his story unless he provides proof that he's Jeremy Tate."

"From what I've heard around town," Amber's mom replied, "half the people are questioning the guy's sanity, and the other half think the whole thing is just a big hoax. Still, the guy was wearing clothes bearing a label from a store that was in business one hundred years ago. So maybe there is some truth to his story. Anyway, that's why some of Tate's relatives—including his grandchildren—will be arriving tonight with old photos of Jeremy Tate."

"Good," Amber said. "Then we'll all find out if this man is who he claims to be."

· · · · · · · · · · ·

That evening Tate's relatives arrived in town, and soon thereafter so did two professors from the University of New Mexico. During the meeting, which was closed to the public, Tate was questioned for hours as experts pored over old photographs of him. The next morning he was given a physical exam and interviewed by two psychiatrists.

Finally, three days later on the six o'clock news, the conclusions of the medical experts, the professors, and Jeremy Tate's distant relatives were made public. Amber and her parents, who along with the rest of the town had become completely absorbed in the whole bizarre thing, gathered expectantly around the TV set in their motel room.

"Topping tonight's broadcast," the anchorwoman began, "is the story of Jeremy Tate. According to experts, old photographs bear some resemblance to the man who made his appearance a short time ago in Doncella, but the photos are fuzzy, cracked, and yellowed with age. The experts and Tate's own relatives, therefore, remain unconvinced.

"Meanwhile, doctors have found the man claiming to be Tate in perfect health, and psychiatric examinations reveal him to be of sound mind, despite his apparent disorientation and increasing confusion. Therefore it is the conclusion of all involved in the case that the man who walked into town one week ago today is an impostor." The newscaster paused for a breath. "After being told of the findings, the man, who was staying at a local hotel, flew into a rage. He is now in seclusion at an undisclosed home in Doncella."

"Well," Amber's father said as the anchorwoman went on to the next story, "I guess that ends that."

···········

Later that night Amber lay in her bed doing everything she could to fall sleep. But all she could think about was the mysterious man who claimed to be Jeremy Tate. The next morning, with only two more days to explore Doncella before their vacation was over, Amber begged her parents to drive out to what had been Tate's ranch. It was only seven miles from their motel, and since her parents were as curious as she was, Amber had no trouble convincing them.

When they got to the ranch several other sightseers were already there. While her parents chatted with them, Amber took a few pictures of the house and the field where Tate had disappeared. But all in all, she and her parents were pretty disappointed in the place. Like the other visitors who had already left, Amber and her parents also decided to go.

"Darn!" Amber's dad exclaimed, as they headed back to the car parked on the other side of the field from where Tate had vanished. "I left my jacket at the ranch house."

100

"I'll go get it," Amber volunteered, heading off at a fast walk right through the tall grass. "Meet you back at the car."

"I left it in the kitchen!" her dad called.

Amber stopped in the middle of the field and looked back at her father. "What?" she called, unaware that she had stopped on the exact spot where Jeremy Tate had vanished over a century ago. She was also unaware that at that exact moment the sun and planets were aligned in precisely the same way they had been when Tate had disappeared.

"I said I left it in—" But her father couldn't finish his sentence. All he could do was stare in shock as his wife let out a wailing scream of disbelief.

Amber had vanished.

···········

Unable to believe her eyes, Amber blinked, then blinked again. "What's going on?" she muttered, totally bewildered.

Shaking her head, Amber slowly walked to where the car and her parents had been. Then she stopped and looked at the remains of the Tate's ranch house. It looked even more weathered than it had earlier, and there wasn't a car or a person in sight.

"Mom! Dad!" Amber yelled. "Where are you?"

The only response was the distant trilling of birds.

*Where'd they go?* She wondered. *Why would they go off and leave me like that?*

Not knowing what else to do, Amber headed off on the seven-mile walk back into town. As she plodded along, she wondered how the weather could have changed so drastically. Shortly before, she and her parents had been wearing jackets, and now it was blistering hot. In fact, by the time she found herself back in town, her face was beet red.

*That's bizarre*, Amber thought, as she made her way down Main Street. Everything—the buildings, cars, and people—looked totally unfamiliar. Determined to figure out what was going on and to find her parents, Amber entered a restaurant and made her way to the counter.

"Hi, I'm Amber Andersen," she said to the waiter, "and I'm looking for—"

"Amber Andersen!" the man blurted, his eyes wide.

"Wh-what's wrong?" Amber asked, noticing that the restaurant had gone dead silent and everybody seemed to be looking at her. As she felt their eyes boring into her back, she also felt a mounting sense of horror as the dawning of a mind-numbing realization hit her. "Someone tell me what's wrong?" she asked again, afraid she knew the answer.

"Fifty years ago," the man said, "a girl named Amber Andersen disappeared right off the face of this earth!"

...........

Within two hours, Amber found herself in the Child Services Center surrounded by doctors, reporters, and curiosity seekers. Earlier she had been taken to a parking lot that had once been the motor lodge she claimed to have stayed in years ago, but it was now a shopping mall. Amber had only been able to stare in shock when she first saw the place. Then she'd burst out sobbing when she'd been told that her father had passed away two years before.

According to what everyone told her, a girl named Amber Andersen—who they still didn't believe she was—

vanished fifty years ago. Crazed with grief, her parents had moved to Doncella in hopes that one day she'd return.

"If you are Amber Andersen, your mother now lives in a retirement home on the outskirts of town," one psychologist explained. And so after she had been "mentally" prepared by social workers and psychiatrists about Mrs. Andersen's ill health, Amber was immediately taken to see the woman who she hoped was indeed her surviving parent.

"Mom!" Amber cried, racing into the small private room.

An elderly woman propped up with pillows in a hospital bed slowly turned her head and looked at Amber with vacant, uncomprehending eyes. "Who are you?" an ancient voice cracked. "And why are you saying I'm your mother?"

••••••••••

The townspeople of Doncella knew the story of Amber Andersen as well as they did that of Jeremy Tate. They listened attentively with both fear and fascination to every word she said, and it became front-page news for days.

In the meantime, medical and dental records were flown in from Amber's hometown in Fresno, California, and a scrapbook found in her mother's room at the retirement home was carefully examined. Experts of every kind, along with media people, traipsed in and out of her room at the Child Services Center until Amber wanted to scream.

Nothing she said seemed to convince anyone that she was telling the truth. And even though all the evidence proved that Amber was the person she said she was, most everyone was convinced that the whole thing was nothing but an elaborate hoax, and she was a fraud.

A few people, however, did believe her. But even they looked at her as if she were some kind of freak and regarded her with fear. Consequently Amber was treated by most as an outcast, especially by the other kids at Child Services. Some of them were even afraid to touch her, as though she had some terrible disease. Heartbroken, confused, her mind in turmoil, Amber spent most of her time alone.

One day a few months after she'd reappeared, Amber was sitting in a park watching kids play on a motorized swingset as people in the street whizzed by in electric-powered cars. It was definately a changed world, and Amber felt certain that she was now destined to be the loneliest person on the planet.

"Going through a hard time, aren't you, miss?" someone asked, walking up and sitting on the bench beside her.

Amber looked over at an elderly man. He looked kind enough, but still she turned away and said nothing. Over the past few months, Amber had learned not to open her mouth for fear of being called crazy or a liar.

"Kind of gets to you," the old man probed. "Feeling all alone in the world, that is." He looked off into the distance, as if deep in thought. "I've been feeling that way since I was twenty-nine."

Amber looked back at the man. "You couldn't possibly know how I feel," she replied sadly.

The elderly man extended his hand. "Oh, yes I would, young lady," he said. "The name's Jeremy Tate."

# The Dead Boy's Clothes

y name is Damon Hodges, and the story you're about to read happened to me and my brother, Eddie. You may accept it as true—which it is—or you may think I made it up. Personally, if somebody told me a story as freaky as this one, I'd have trouble believing it. Still, like I said, every word is true.

It all started on the day after Eddie's twelfth birthday, April 19, during spring vacation. It was a Sunday, and that morning Eddie and I went over to the park to shoot some baskets. Eddie was wearing all the clothes he'd gotten for his birthday—a Chicago Bears T-shirt, a Minnesota Vikings jacket, and the kind of basketball shoes the pros wear. Since money's been a little tight lately for our family, Mom and

Dad got all of Eddie's stuff at a thrift shop. But he didn't care; it looked practically brand new.

Anyway, Eddie had just taken off his purple jacket and we had just started shooting a few hoops when the horror began. I drove in and did a lay-up, then whipped the ball back to Eddie. He caught it and was on a dribble-drive toward the basket when he let out a yelp.

"My hands are bleeding!" he cried. He dropped the ball and it bounced away, spattering blood all over the court.

"What happened?" I asked, hurrying over to Eddie. I thought that it was my fault, that somehow I'd thrown the ball so hard that it had cut my brother's hands. But when we examined his bloody palms, we found a bunch of weird, deep gashes—not the kind he could have gotten from merely catching a basketball but the kind of cuts you'd get if you fell on broken glass or sharp rocks.

"What happened?" Eddie cried, wincing in pain.

"Got me," I said with a shrug, trying to stay calm.

Shaking his head as if trying to clear it, Eddie told me he was going to wash off the blood, and I followed him over to the drinking fountain. Blood was everywhere, and I had to dodge the blood that was now literally dripping from his hands. I could tell that Eddie was pretty freaked out by the whole thing, and so was I, but what I saw after he'd washed off all the blood *really* gave me the chills. There wasn't a single scratch on Eddie's hands once the blood was gone. I mean, his palms suddenly didn't have a scratch on them!

"I don't get it," Eddie said. "Where are the cuts? Was it just my imagination?"

"I saw the cuts too," I said, staring at his now unharmed hands. "At least I *think* I did. Do your hands still hurt?"

"Not anymore," he replied. "And there's no trace of—"

Suddenly Eddie let out a cry of pain and grabbed his left arm. As if a giant invisible cat was dragging invisible claws across his skin in slow motion, the flesh on Eddie's arm was ripping open right before our eyes.

"What's happening to me?" Eddie screamed, dancing around in pain until he finally fell to his knees, crying.

"I—I don't know!" I stammered. "I mean, I've never seen anything like it. Come on, let's go home!"

Eddie and I ran toward our house, only about half a mile from the park. But before we got there the blood on Eddie's arm had completely dried up. Then it just disappeared, like the moisture on a fogged-up windshield does when you turn on the defroster. The clawlike scratches also vanished, sort of like some weird special-effect from a movie . . . only this was for real!

Eddie was fighting back tears. "Why is this happening, Damon?" he repeated as we made our way to our house.

"I don't know," was all I could say.

The second we stepped through the front door Eddie started shrieking again. He was rolling around on the carpet, this time clutching his leg. I knelt beside him, then was about to go find our parents when Mom came rushing through the back door. "Eddie! Damon! What's wrong?" she yelled, hurrying in with a gardening trowel in hand.

Dad came rushing down the stairs. "What's all the commotion?" he asked. When he saw Eddie on the floor, our father ran to his side.

"I think my ankle's sprained," Eddie groaned, writhing around and holding his leg.

"Did you hurt yourself playing basketball?" Mom asked.

"Mom," I said, answering for him, "this has nothing to do with basketball. Nothing at all. Something really weird is happening to Eddie."

"What do you mean, weird?" Dad asked, a skeptical look on his face as he bent over my brother.

Eddie and I babbled out the whole story, but as we spoke I could tell neither of my parents believed us. I could hardly blame them for thinking we'd made the whole thing up. After all, the story was pretty wild.

"Yeah, sure, guys," Dad said, one eyebrow raised. "Did you ever think of writing scary stories?"

"No, listen," I began to get a little upset. "It really hap—"

"Let's get you off that ankle, Eddie," Mom said, cutting me off. "And, Damon, this is no time to be telling stories."

I stared at Eddie. It looked like he was about to pass out from the pain, and I felt like I was going to explode with frustration. At least for now it appeared the best thing I could do for my brother was help my dad get him upstairs.

"I'll bring up some ice right away, Eddie," Mom called after us, as if the only thing wrong with him was an ordinary sprain. But I knew there was definitely something else wrong with my brother, something ice wouldn't fix.

Once we got Eddie into the room we shared, Dad took off Eddie's shoes and took a look at his ankle. It was already pretty badly swollen . . . at least it was until after Mom brought up the ice. Dad wrapped it in an ace bandage, and the two of them left the room. That's when Eddie's eyes grew wide with fear.

"Look at this, Damon," he said in a chilling whisper as he tossed the ice pack aside and then unwrapped his ankle.

The swelling had completely disappeared.

"This is crazy," I said, shaking my head. "I don't get it."

"That makes two of us!" Eddie replied, twisting his ankle around. "Look—it doesn't even hurt anymore." He shrugged, then pulled off his new T-shirt. "Listen, I think I'll take a shower," he said over his shoulder as he headed for the bathroom without even a trace of a hobble. "A *cold* one. It might wake me up from this—" Suddenly he stopped in his tracks and slapped himself on the forehead. "What an idiot I am!" he exclaimed. "I left my new jacket at the park!"

He came back into the room and started slipping back into his T-shirt when I told him that I'd get his jacket for him. I flew out of the house and ran almost the whole way to the park. I wanted something to go right for my brother today. I wanted to bring him his jacket and pretend like nothing bad had ever happened.

But my heart sank as I reached the basketball courts. The jacket was gone. I looked everywhere—including the lost and found—before I headed home with the bad news.

. . . . . . . . . . .

Nothing else happened the rest of the day. But as if everything hadn't been bad enough, now Eddie was really bummed about losing his jacket, and both of us just sat around trying to figure out some sort of explanation for all the mysterious injuries happening to Eddie.

Our parents seemed unconcerned and still didn't believe our story. Although Eddie had shown them how his ankle had miraculously healed, they just told him he was lucky the ice worked so quickly. On top of that, they even got angry at Eddie for losing his new jacket.

Just wanting to forget the whole thing, Eddie and I spent the rest of the afternoon playing chess.

That night it took me a while to get to sleep. We have bunk beds, and Eddie, who has the lower bunk, was snoring so loudly I thought I'd never doze off, but eventually I did.

It was about 3:00 A.M. when something woke me up. I heard a creaking noise, and all bleary-eyed, I looked from our bedroom clock to Eddie, who was standing at the window with his back to me.

"Hey, Eddie," I said. "What're you doing?"

He didn't answer, and I started to feel really spooked, wondering what he was up to. "Eddie, come on. Cut it out."

"Huh?" a groggy voice from the bunk below me croaked.

Electric fear went up my spine as I looked over the edge of my bed . . . at Eddie!

"Whaddya want?" he mumbled from the bed. Then I heard my brother suck in his breath as he turned his head and saw that we were not alone.

"Wh-who are you?" Eddie stammered at the shadowy being now looking right at him.

The figure slowly lifted its arms toward Eddie. "Griffin Bernau," the voice of a young boy answered, his words hollow like whispers in a tomb. He paused for a moment. "Give them back," he demanded.

"G-give wh-what back?" Eddie asked, sounding as though he were about to scream.

Suddenly, as though lit up inside by a bright, pinkish light, a boy appeared where the shadow had been. But he was there only briefly before he shrank to the size of a doll, then to nothing but a dot of light that eventually disappeared altogether.

For a split second Eddie and I looked at each other in complete shock. Then our voices joined together in a single, piercing scream that filled the entire house.

●●●●●●●●●●●

We were up the rest of the night, shaking like leaves. And our parents were a little scared too. Although they tried to dismiss the whole thing as a case of our overactive imaginations, our shrieks in the middle of the night had them pretty shaken up. They also had no explanation why Eddie and I *both* had seen and heard the exact same thing.

"He said his name was Griffin Bernau, or something like that," Eddie told our parents for about the third time. "And he wanted something back."

"Do you know a kid named Griffin Bernau or any family around here by that name?" I asked. "Do you think you could help us find out who he is?"

Neither of our parents knew anyone by that name, but they both promised that they would try to find out in the morning, and true to their word, they did.

At about 7:00 A.M. Dad called the police station, but the desk sergeant he talked to didn't recognize the name Griffin Bernau, and he didn't have time to check into it right then. He did tell my dad that a convicted murderer had escaped a couple of days before and had been reported seen in our area, but the guy's name was George Ember.

Mom and Dad made a couple more calls but got no information, and finally they had to give up and go to work. Worried about the news regarding the escaped convict, they told Eddie and me we had to stay indoors. Eddie didn't seem to mind—I guess he was afraid more weird stuff was going to happen to him—but I was pretty bummed. After all, it was a sunny day, and we only had a few days left of spring break before we had to go back to school.

Anyway, Eddie kicked back on the sofa and flicked on the TV, and I looked at him like he was crazy. How could he act like nothing had happened? I mean it's not every day that some ghostly kid shows up in your bedroom.

And then an idea hit me.

"I'm going to call Katie Klein," I told him, picking up the cordless phone on the coffee table.

Eddie looked up half-interested. "Really? I didn't know you liked her."

"I don't," I said, a little annoyed that he was ignoring this whole thing. "Her dad's a reporter. Maybe he knows something about Griffin Bernau. You know, like maybe some accident or something involving him."

"Yeah, check it out," Eddie said, finally taking his eyes off the dumb movie he'd been watching.

As it turned out, Katie didn't even have to ask her dad about Griffin Bernau. She already knew all about the guy. In fact, she'd met his parents when they'd come into the thrift shop where she helps out. It was Charity Thrift, the same place my parents had gotten all of Eddie's birthday stuff.

"It's kind of a sad story," Katie said. Then she went on and told me all about Griffin Bernau. As I listened, the hair stood up on the back of my neck, and by the time I hung up my hands were trembling.

"What'd she say?" Eddie asked me. "You look freaked."

I started to tell him what Katie had told me, but just then he opened his mouth to let out a blood-curdling shriek.

Horrified, I watched as he pulled up the front of his Bears T-shirt to reveal a dark purple bruise. It looked like ink had spilled all over his chest and was now being absorbed right into his skin.

"Damon, help me!" he cried. And as he reached out to me I heard the bones of his right wrist snap.

Rushing over to him, my heart beating with terror, I tried to rip the clothes right off my brother. For after hearing Katie's story I knew that *they* were the cause of Eddie's pain.

"You've got to take off everything you got from that thrift store!" I yelled, dropping to my knees and pulling at one of his basketball sneakers.

But Eddie didn't respond. Instead, a horrible gurgling sound came from him, and then he opened his mouth wide to scream . . . except water came pouring out!

"It's the clothes!" I screamed, struggling with the laces of his other shoe. "They're Griffin Bernau's! That's what he wants back!"

But by then Eddie had gone limp and his eyes had rolled back in his head. Realizing that my only hope was to continue to pull off those terrible clothes, I literally tore the T-shirt right off him.

It was like a miracle. Instantly Eddie began breathing normally, the bones in his broken wrist reset themselves, and the bruise on his chest began to shrink from sight.

"Y-you were wearing the clothes of a dead boy!" I told Eddie, my voice quavering. "Griffin Bernau died a couple of weeks ago. He was canoeing alone at Porter Lake when he accidentally tipped over. It was a horrible accident," I went on. "He was sucked into one of the drains in the dam and by the time they found him, his body was all beaten up. He had cuts all over his hands, scratches all over his arms, a twisted ankle . . . and a broken wrist!"

"All the things that happened to me!" Eddie exclaimed.

"Katie said that Griffin's parents told her he liked to wear the gear of his favorite sports teams. Anyway, when he died they donated a lot of his stuff to the same thrift shop where Mom and Dad bought your birthday presents."

"But how could wearing . . . " Eddie began.

"I don't know," I said. "But one thing I *do* know—Griffin wants his clothes back."

············

That afternoon, Eddie and I went to the cemetery. We found Griffin Bernau's grave and put his clothes beside it. Then we returned home and mostly just sat there.

Finally we turned on the TV and were watching some dumb game show, when a special news bulletin came on. The escaped convict had been located in the next county. He was dead when the police found him, and investigators have been baffled ever since.

You see, they found the car he'd been driving pulled off to the side of the road. There wasn't a lake or stream or river anywhere nearby, but slumped behind the wheel was the convict . . . his lungs completely filled with water. The police didn't understand at all what had happened, and they didn't see the connection between how the man had died and the purple football jacket he was wearing.

# Monster Bait

E xcept for being a little homesick, Barbara was having the time of her life. The adventuresome fourteen-year-old had arrived the night before at the home of her uncle Kyle and cousin Megan, who lived on the outskirts of Glenwick, Scotland. Barbara was going to stay with them for the next two weeks while her parents enjoyed a second honeymoon in Mexico.

"Tell me all about the Loch Ness Monster," she urged Megan as they hiked the trail down to the lake where the creature supposedly had been sighted. "I read that some people think it's some kind of giant eel."

Megan chuckled and tossed her red curls. "Yes, and others think Nessie is a huge wormlike dinosaur left over from prehistoric times. To me, the whole idea of a monster is just a silly myth," she said in her lilting Scottish accent. "Anyway, it's sure grown to be one of the biggest tourist attractions in the world."

"Really?" Barbara asked. "I've heard that lots of people have actually taken photos of the monster. I was sort of hoping I might take one myself."

Megan rolled her eyes. "All the photos are fake, I assure you, and the people who claim to have taken them are just phonies looking to make money. In fact, if you ask me, I'm tired of all the silly stories that've been made up about this sea serpent, or whatever it's supposed to be, and I wouldn't mind if I never heard another one."

"You're probably right," Barbara said, a note of disappointment in her voice as she followed her freckle-faced cousin down a rocky slope.

A few moments later the lake came into view, and Megan stopped and pointed at the desolate gray water shrouded in a cold mist. "Well, there's the most famous lake in the world, Loch Ness," Megan announced.

Barbara shrugged. "I guess the monster isn't in today," she said, snapping a few pictures anyway. "Can we get a little closer to the water?" she asked.

"Sure," Megan said with a smile. "But there still won't be any serpent."

The two cousins made their way down to the shore. Approaching the water, Megan pointed out the brown scum on the surface and tiny mounds of the stuff that had washed up onto the sand. "That's peat moss," she explained. "When it rains, the moss washes down from the surrounding mountains into the *loch*, which is Scottish for lake."

Barbara was stepping over a clump of the stuff when she was suddenly startled by a splash and a little geyser popping up from the water.

Megan groaned. "Oh, don't worry. It's just the stupid McHufferney twins." She gazed off toward the surrounding hillside. "They're always out there trying to scare tourists with their stupid pranks."

Suddenly a barrage of rocks came flying right from the general area Megan was looking at. Most landed in the lake, but one accidentally glanced off Megan's scalp causing a trickle of blood to run down her cheek.

"Get outta here, you disgusting oafs!" Megan shouted, wiping the blood. "Ya hit me, ya dumb fools!"

"Are you OK?" Barbara asked, as two scraggly looking boys scrambled noisily out of the bushes, then headed off laughing like hyenas.

"It's just a tiny scratch," Megan replied. "I'll be fine. But we should leave before those idiots come back."

Together Barbara and Megan hurried along the shore of the lake, completely draped in a hazy curtain of fog. Coming to a cluster of small boulders, they were about to sit down and take a rest when suddenly the hair stood up on Barbara's neck.

"Megan, look!" she cried, excitement and terror making her voice rise a full octive.

Megan's eyes followed Barbara's trembling finger, then her face turned white. "It's not possible!" she muttered, her mouth dropping open in disbelief.

Slowly, their eyes opened wide, the two girls approached a huge reptilian creature lying half on the shore and half in the icy water of the lake.

"Is . . . is it the monster?" Barbara asked.

"It has to be!" Megan exclaimed. "Just look at the size of her. It's Nessie, all right. I never thought all the stories were true, but this has to be the Loch Ness Monster!" A sad look came over Megan's face. "Gosh, the old girl looks sick, doesn't she?"

It was all Barbara could do to keep from running away, but she had to admit her cousin was right. The monster did look sick, and for that matter, kind of helpless.

Mustering every ounce of courage they had, the two girls slowly approached the huge creature lying motionless on the beach. It was a spongy white color, and along the back of its heavy, snakelike body—which looked almost the size of a school bus—were several humps, or dorsal fins. Its long, looping tail lay half-submerged in the opaque water.

"Is it dead?" Barbara asked.

Megan nodded. "It sure looks that way."

"The poor thing has probably beached itself," Barbara commented. "Sick whales will do that sometimes, so why not sick sea monsters?"

The two girls stood in silence for a moment, staring at the still beast. Then Barbara shuddered. Peering closer, she bent over the creature, and with a trembling hand she touched its head.

"Yech!" she squealed. "It feels like . . . rubber!"

"It's so amazing," Megan said, stepping next to Barbara. "I mean, all these years people have been saying Nessie is a monster, but this creature isn't monstrous at all—it's almost . . . beautiful!"

Growing braver, Barbara passed her hand near the three slits in the side of the creature's neck. "These must be its gills," she said. And then, to her surprise, she felt warm, humid air on her palm. "I think it's still breathing!" she exclaimed. "It must be—"

"Watch out!" Megan screamed, jumping back and pulling Barbara with her. "That means it's alive!"

Clutching each other, almost falling down, the two cousins scrambled away from the gigantic creature and stared at its mouth, now slowly opening to expose rows and rows of curved, oversized fangs. A black, forked tongue flickered between the fangs as a deep, gurgling hiss escaped the reviving beast, whose eyes slowly opened and fixed on the two trembling girls.

"Look at her eyes!" Barbara gasped. "They're . . . like . . . *intelligent!* And almost human-looking!"

"My goodness!" Megan cried. "Nessie's like a person locked inside a monster. And it looks like she's asking us to help her."

"Poor thing," Barbara said sadly. "I wish we *could* help her. But how?"

"Come on," Megan said, already taking off. "Let's go tell my dad. He'll know what to do."

Before following her cousin, Barbara took several quick shots of the dying creature with her camera. Then she whispered, "Good-bye, Nessie, old girl," and hurried away at a fast jog.

...........

Five years before, Megan's father had suffered a spinal injury in a fall from the roof of the cottage in which he and Megan lived. Mostly confined to a wheelchair, he did get around with crutches and leg braces when he needed to. And since he and Megan's mother, who had died of cancer when Megan was only five years old, met as tourists at Loch Ness, when he heard Megan and Barbara's story he was determined that nothing would keep him from seeing the fabled monster.

Slowly and with considerable difficulty, Megan's dad followed the two girls back to the lake. But when they finally reached the site where the creature lay, their hearts sank. Totally limp now, her head and long, tapering neck draped on shore, her body half-submerged in the lapping water, Nessie was surrounded by flies . . . not to mention a large gathering of curious, insensitive humans.

The McHufferney boys, who had thrown rocks at Barbara and Megan earlier that day, were among the crowd laughing and prodding at the beached creature along with the rest. It was an ugly sight—dozens of uncaring people gawking and taking pictures of the dead legendary beast.

"Leave the poor thing in peace!" Megan yelled.

"Ah, get outta here!" a sloppy teenage girl sneered. "We were here first!"

"It's us who found the beast," a man with long hair and yellow teeth growled. "The thing belongs to *us* now. We'll do as we please!"

"We're all going to be rich and famous!" a woman with dirty blond hair yelled. "So don't you be thinking of nosing in on what's ours!"

Shaking their heads at the sorry sight before them, Megan, Barbara, and Uncle Kyle watched as the people, one after the other, posed with the monster. Some posed with one foot on the monster and their arms crossed over their chest as though they'd just caught Nessie, while others straddled the poor creature as though riding a dead reptilian horse. The whole thing made Barbara sick.

"What's wrong with you people?" she screamed. "Haven't you got any feelings?"

"There's your answer," Megan said angrily. "Just look at them. They're nothing but a bunch of ghouls!"

"You watch what you say!" one of the McHufferney twins threatened, leering as he approached menacingly. "Or you can bet you'll be sorry."

Megan, Barbara, and her uncle backed away.

"We'd better get out of here," Uncle Kyle said. "There's no telling what this bunch will do. *They're* the monsters here. Anyway, we should notify the authorities—and professors and scientists at the university. They'll want to know that Nessie's been found."

Barbara was just about to turn away with her uncle and cousin when she decided to take a couple of quick pictures. But no sooner had she raised the camera to her eye than she felt a hand grab hold of her wrist.

"What do you think you're doing?" a grubby-looking boy demanded as he grabbed Barbara's camera and tossed it to the sloppy girl. "Trying to butt in on our find of the century, weren't ya?"

"Give me my camera back!" Barbara yelled.

"Oh, now look what I've done," the terrible girl said with a laugh as she opened the camera and pulled out the film. Then snickering, she said, "Oops!" and tossed the camera into the lake.

Barbara was in a rage. Not only had she lost the first pictures she'd taken of the dying Loch Ness Monster, but she'd also lost the camera her parents had given to her as a birthday present. With nothing left to do, she simply burst into tears of frustration.

"I'm so sorry," Megan said, walking up and putting an arm around her cousin. "I wish I could make it up to you, but I can't—any more than I can put brains in these stupid people's heads."

Barbara looked from the leering, laughing faces of the people to the poor creature on the beach. For a moment she wished that it could somehow recover long enough to avenge itself—*and* her.

"Let's go, girls," Uncle Kyle said, maneuvering on his crutches up the shore. "Like I said, it's these people who are the *real* monsters!"

Wiping the tears from her face, Barbara nodded and headed away. But the three of them had taken only a few steps when they heard the people behind them scream in unison. "It's alive!"

Whipping around, Barbara stared in disbelief. Nessie's eyes had opened! Then, in a great heaving motion, the monster's neck lifted and its head rose.

Terrified, everyone who had been torturing the beast now backed away. But it was no use. They were all trapped by a steep cliff directly behind them.

In horror, Barbara, Megan, and Uncle Kyle watched as Nessie came closer on her huge, scalloped flippers. It was an incredible sight, and Barbara couldn't believe her eyes. It looked as though the creature was inspecting each person in turn. Then, with its tongue flickering, it reared back its tapering head and let forth a bellowing cry that reverberated across the lake.

"L-look!" Megan stammered, pointing out across the water. There, along the surface of the dark, desolate lake, was a great, long ripple of movement as though something was swimming just below the surface at a rapid speed . . . and it was heading straight for the shore!

"It can't be!" Uncle Kyle exclaimed.

"There are two Loch Ness monsters!" Megan cried.

But Barbara just stood there shaking her head. "No, there aren't!" she gasped, spellbound by what she was seeing. "There are hundreds!"

Sure enough, streaming toward the shore were countless numbers of black, slithering forms headed right for them!

Petrified, Megan, Barbara, and Uncle Kyle stood rooted to the spot, watching in awe as Nessie, who had kept an eye on the people who had tortured her, waited for her fellow monsters. It was as though she had decided to hold those people captive while allowing Barbara, Megan, and Uncle Kyle to go free.

"Let's get outta here!" Megan cried. "I think Nessie's letting us go!"

But already the other creatures were fast approaching the shore. It looked as though the lake had literally come alive with hundreds of huge, serpentine reptiles, their long, looping necks arching out of the water. Then all at once, they emerged, and with their mouths opened wide, their enormous, scale-covered bodies glistening, they slithered everywhere onto the beach.

"Noooo!" Barbara shrieked, certain that at any second she would be devoured by one of the writhing creatures.

But whenever any came near her, Nessie let out a snarling bellow of warning. Instead of attacking Barbara, her uncle, or her cousin, Nessie actually seemed to be guarding them!

The McHufferney boys and the others, however, had no chance. For a few brief moments, the shore was a writhing tangle of humans and avenging serpents. Then, as quickly as they had come, the reptiles were gone . . . taking their human "snacks" with them.

Nessie, too, was about to plunge back into the lake. But before she did, she gave Barbara, Megan, and Uncle Kyle a last look as if to say thanks. Then, with one fluid movement, she slid into the dark waters of the Loch Ness, and disappeared into the mist.

All at once the shores were empty and *very* quiet. Not a trace of the twins or any of the heartless people who had tortured Nessie remained.

For a long while Barbara, Megan, and Uncle Kyle stood together in silence.

"Incredible," Uncle Kyle finally muttered, his voice trembling. "Nessie was just pretending to be dead."

"You know what she was doing, don't you?" Megan asked Barbara.

Barbara nodded, her eyes still fixed on the water. "Uh huh," she muttered. "Nessie was just acting as bait."

"I think you're right, lassie," Uncle Kyle said. "But there's one thing I don't understand," he added, a puzzled look on his face. "Why do you suppose Nessie and the others left us alone? I mean, do you think it's because we weren't cruel to her?"

"I think it's because somehow Nessie knew we stood up for her," Megan said.

"And so she stood up for us," Barbara added.

"Incredible," Uncle Kyle commented as the three headed up the shore. Absolutely incredible."

The loch was now quiet, with only a few flecks of foam left to show that anything had happened. As the foam disintegrated and disappeared, for an instant the silhouettes of huge wriggling forms could be seen beneath the surface. They too disappeared, and then there was nothing but the dark, silent waters of the lake . . . and its secret world below.

# COLLECT ALL THE SCARES YOU'VE EVER DREAMED OF AT YOUR FAVORITE BOOKSTORE!

If you are unable to find these titles at your bookstore, fill in the Quantity Column for each title described, and order directly from Price Stern Sloan.

Mail order form to:
PUTNAM PUBLISHING GROUP
Mail Order Department
Department B
P.O. Box 12289
Newark, NJ 07101-5289

FAX (201) 933-2316
☎ (800) 788-6262
☎ (201) 933-9292
On a touch-tone phone, hit prompt 1

## Collect all the terrifying titles in the Scary Stories for Sleep-Overs series . . .

| ISBN # | Quantity | Title | US price | Can. price |
|---|---|---|---|---|
| 0-8431-2914-X | _____ | Scary Stories for Sleep-Overs | $4.95 | $6.50 |
| 0-8431-3451-8 | _____ | More Scary Stories for Sleep-Overs | $4.95 | $6.50 |
| 0-8431-3588-3 | _____ | Still More Scary Stories for Sleep-Overs | $4.95 | $6.50 |
| 0-8431-3746-0 | _____ | Even More Scary Stories for Sleep-Overs | $4.95 | $6.50 |
| 0-8431-3915-3 | _____ | Super Scary Stories for Sleep-Overs | $4.95 | $6.75 |
| 0-8431-3916-1 | _____ | More Super Scary Stories for Sleep-Overs | $4.95 | $6.75 |
| 0-8431-8219-9 | _____ | Mega Scary Stories for Sleep-Overs | $5.95 | $7.95 |

## And check out the titles in this brand new scary and spine-tingling series . . .

| ISBN # | Quantity | Title | US price | Can. price |
|---|---|---|---|---|
| 0-8431-8220-2 | _____ | Scary Mysteries for Sleep-Overs | $5.95 | $7.95 |
| 0-8431-8221-0 | _____ | More Scary Mysteries for Sleep-Overs | $5.95 | $7.95 |

## Now dive into Nightmares! How Will Yours End? — Each title has over 20 endings!

| ISBN # | Quantity | Title | US price | Can. price |
|---|---|---|---|---|
| 0-8431-3862-9 | _____ | Castle of Horror | $4.50 | $5.95 |
| 0-8431-3861-0 | _____ | Cave of Fear | $4.50 | $5.95 |
| 0-8431-3860-2 | _____ | Planet of Terror | $4.50 | $5.95 |
| 0-8431-3863-7 | _____ | Valley of the Screaming Statues | $4.50 | $5.95 |

**All orders must be prepaid in US funds**

❏ Check or Money Order
❏ Visa
❏ Mastercard-Interbank
❏ American Express
❏ International Money Order or Bank Draft

Expiration Date _____

Signature _____

Daytime phone #_____

**Postage/Handling Charges as Follows:**

$2.50 for first book
$0.75 each additional book
(Maximum shipping charge of $6.25)

| | |
|---|---|
| Merchandise total | $_____ |
| Shipping/Handling | $_____ |
| Applicable Sales Tax (CA, NJ, NY, VA) | $_____ |
| GST (Canada) | $_____ |
| Total Amount (US currency only) | $_____ |

**Minimum order $15.00**

NOTE: Prices and handling charges are subject to change without notice, but we will always ship the least expensive edition available. Please allow 4 to 6 weeks for delivery.

**Refer to source: SCARY**